哈福

哈福

哈福

Spoken American English

1分鐘快聽學習法

躺著學美國口語1000

用TED名師的方法，美語馬上聊不停

蘇盈盈 · Lily Thomas —— 合著

哈福

用 TED 名師的方法，美語馬上聊不停

　　翻開本書，你一定會發現，這本書太簡單了！沒錯，本書就是那麼易學的一本書，真的可以躺著聽、躺著學！

　　學好英語的最佳入門法則，就是找對老師、找對教材。有鑑於英語已成為全球人士必學的國際語言，華裔美籍人士蘇盈盈小姐及專業英語教學老師 Lily Thomas 兩人共同合作，特別為亞洲人共同精心策畫了這本書。

　　這是一本專門針對有中學程度，英語只學過初、中級的人所撰寫，作者將她們在美國成長、生活、所見所聞，以最簡單的詞彙，將常用美語的句型、文法，融會在情境會話中。

　　全書沒有冗長的文法解說，所引用的常用語都是熱門字眼，只要一書在手，在家就可以擁有「一個好老師」、「一本好教材」，不用再苦苦思量、舌頭打結，學過多年英語的你，會恍然大悟，原來英語可以這麼輕輕鬆鬆就說出口。

進步的現代科技是學習語言者最大的福音之一，本書搭配有精製的 MP3，讓你利用 MP3，達到一級棒的學習效果。

聽各行各業傑出人物在 TED 中的演講，是我每天的功課和習慣，其中令我最敬佩的，就是英語名師在 TED 的演講中提到：1000 單，就含蓋了 85% 會話必備單字。

5 個方法、6 個原則，6 個月就能學會英語。好東西要和好朋友分享，在這裡特別推薦給有心想學英語的讀者。

你是不是常有這樣的困擾：

單字、片語、口語、會話，背了又背，碰到老外還是開不了口？

其實，你可以不用那麼累。

記住英語名師在 TED 的演講，你真的可以躺著學，輕鬆說。

456 英語學習秘技即是：

4 個捷徑、5 個方法，6 個月快速溜美語

【速記好學，4 捷徑】大的優點

1. 超好學：用最簡單的字，花最少的時間，說最道地的美語，每一句都是美國人生活中最常用的口語。

2. 易學好記：每句口語都是最熱門的字眼，字字簡單，句句簡短，一看就懂，即使只有初級程度，也能說一口超強美國話。

3.一招半式闖江湖：省時省力，是學習英語的成功拍檔，見到老外，勇往直前，放心大膽去「talk」「talk」。

4.躺著聽、躺著學：隨時隨地，跟聽、跟説，是學好純正美語最佳捷徑。

【輕鬆學會，5方法】

1.**專注**：專注於你有興趣的那種美語內容。

2.**溝通**：把美語當作溝通工具使用。

3.**聊天**：不要從英語中猜意思，而要從交流中了解意思。

4.**大腦**：訓練你的大腦，讓它接受美語的聲調。

5.**心情**：高興、放鬆、好奇，您會很快學好美語。

【實力倍增，6原則】

1.**常用口語**：學美語，記 80 句重點口語，就已含蓋了日常會話 85% 的內容。

2.**大量聽**：躺著背、躺著學、躺著聽、坐著聽、開車聽、走路聽，最好。

3.**大量學**：只要會 10 個動詞、名詞和形容詞，再擴充和聯想，就能脫口説出 1000 句會話。

4.**專注**：學美語專注於理解意思，要優先於理解單詞。

5.**模仿**：學美語，一定要模仿老外的面部表情和面部運

動。

　　6. 左右腦圖像記憶：連接大腦圖像記憶和聯想法，印象
會較深刻，而且長久喔。

　　什麼是學語言最好、最有效的方法，相信每個人的答案
和經驗都不一樣。因為每個人的學習習慣並不盡相同，吸收
能力也不一樣。有些人喜歡到當地學習、有些人喜歡啃文法
書、有些人喜歡嘗試新奇獨特的方法，體驗與眾不同的學習
方式。其實不管哪一種方法，自己吸收的效果好，就是最有
效的學習方式。

　　本書特別精選了，初學英語必學的 80 句口語、1000 句
會話。這些口語和會話都是最簡單、最初級、最實用的會話。
為了讓讀者免於死背的痛苦，每一個單字都很簡單，馬上學
馬上會，馬上可以和老外聊不停。

編者　謹識

CONTENTS

Allow me.
請讓我來。

當對方並沒有提出要求,而你主動提出要幫忙對方時,就說「Allow me.」這是一句很有紳士風度、很有禮貌的説法,大都是男士對女士説的。

好說好用 1

W: I need to open this jar.
我必須打開這個罐子。

M: Allow me.
讓我來。

W: Wow, you're really strong.
哇,你好強壯。

M: No, it wasn't on there that tight.
不是的,蓋子並沒蓋得很緊。

好說好用 2

M: Will you allow me to escort you to the dance?
你願意讓我陪伴你去參加舞會嗎?

W: You bet.
好的。

M: Where would you like to go after the dance?
舞會後你想去哪裡?

W: How about to Seafood King?
去「海鮮大王」怎麼樣？

M: That sounds good.
聽起來是個好主意。

W: Great, it's a date.
好，就這麼說定了。

好說好用 3

W: Allow me to get the door for you.
讓我替你開門。

M: Thank you.
謝謝你。

W: No problem.
沒問題。

M: You are very nice.
你人真好。

單字慣用語

☑ jar	[dʒɑr]	罐子	
☑ tight	[taɪt]	緊	
☑ escort	[ɪˈskɔrt]	護送	
☑ allow	[əˈlaʊ]	允許	
☑ You bet.		好的。	
☑ No problem.		沒問題。	
☑ It's a date.		就這麼說定。	

Anything you say.
好的。

 MP3-3

易 開 竅

「Anything you say.」是「好的。」或「你怎麼說,我怎麼做。」的意思。有人請你幫個忙、做件事,你可以回答「Anything you say.」有人問你要做什麼,你也可以回答「Anything you say.」。

好說好用 1

W: Will you hand me that towel?
請你把那條毛巾遞過來好嗎?

M: Sure, anything you say.
好的,沒問題。

W: Thank you.
謝謝你。

M: You're welcome.
不客氣。

好說好用 2

M: What are we going to do today?
你今天要做什麼。

W: Anything you say.
隨便你。

M: Let's go to the beach.
讓我們到海邊去。

W: Good idea.
好主意。

M: Do you have your swimsuit with you?
你的泳衣有沒有帶在身邊？

W: No, it is at home.
沒有，放在家裡。

好說好用 3

W: Get to work.
去工作。

M: Anything you say, boss.
是的，老闆。

W: Don't forget that.
別忘了。

M: I won't.
我不會忘的。

單字慣用語

☑ hand	[hænd]	v. 遞過來
☑ towel	[taʊl]	毛巾
☑ beach	[bitʃ]	海邊
☑ swimsuit	[ˈswɪmsut]	游泳衣
☑ boss	[bɔs]	老闆
☑ You're welcome.		不用客氣。

Are you ready for this?
你有心理準備嗎？

易 開 竅

 MP3-4

當你想要告訴對方一件不尋常的消息時，可以先説句「Are you ready for this?」讓對方有個心理準備，來聽一個會令他吃驚的消息。

好說好用 1

M: What's going on?
什麼事？

W: Are you ready for this?
你有心理準備嗎？

M: What?
是什麼事？

W: Mary and John are going steady.
瑪麗和約翰兩人很要好。

M: You're joking.
你在開玩笑吧。

W: No, they just told me.
沒有，他們剛剛告訴我的。

好說好用 2

W: Are you ready for this?
你有心理準備嗎？

M: Ready for what?
準備什麼事？

W: I got an A on my Math test.
我的數學考試成績得到 A。

M: No way!
不可能的！

好說好用 3

M: Hey, are you ready for this one?
嘿，你有心理準備嗎？

W: What?
什麼事？

M: I heard John Lin has a crush on you.
我聽說林約翰很喜歡妳。

W: Is that so?
真的嗎？

單字慣用語

☑ steady	['stɛdɪ]	固定
☑ joking	['dʒokɪŋ]	開玩笑
☑ test	[tɛst]	測驗
☑ crush	[krʌʃ]	（口語）熱戀
☑ go steady		做固定的男女朋友
☑ has a crush on...		喜歡上某人

As I see it...
依我看……

🔘 *MP3-5*

易開竅

想要表示你的看法或意見時，可以先説「As I see it.」，再説你想説的事。

好説好用 1

W: As I see it, you owe me $20.
我説，你欠我二十元。

M: Well, I don't see it that way.
嘿，我的看法可不是這樣。

W: You should.
你應該這麼看的。

M: I don't owe you a dime.
我沒欠你一毛錢。

W: Yes, you do.
有的，你有。

M: For what?
為什麼欠你？

好説好用 2

M: Who are you voting for class president?
你要選誰做班代表？

W: As I see it, John is the only worthy candidate.
依我看，約翰是唯一值得的人選。

M: I disagree, I am voting for Mary.
我不同意，我要選瑪麗。

W: I can't believe you are voting for her.
我真不相信你要選她。

好說好用 3

W: Who do you think will win the Superbowl this year?
你認為今年誰會贏得超級杯？

M: The Dallas Cowboys will win again, as I see it.
依我看，達拉斯的牛仔隊會贏。

W: No, they are going to lose.
不，他們會輸。

M: What makes you think that?
你怎麼會這麼想？

W: It's their turn to lose.
輪到他們輸了。

M: You're wrong.
你錯了。

單字慣用語

☑ owe [o] 欠

☑ dime [daɪm] 十分錢

☑ voting [ˈvotɪŋ] 投票
（vote 的現在分詞）

☑ worthy [ˈwɝðɪ] 值得的

☑ candidate [ˈkændɪˌdet] 候選人

☑ disagree [ˌdɪsəˈgri] 不同意

☑ turn [tɝn] n. 輪流

☑ vote for 投票給（某人）

MEMO

Call again.
以後再打來。

 MP3-6

易開罐

「Call again.」是指以後再打一次電話。說這句話的情形有三種可能：對方要找的人不在，你請他以後再打來；或是某人又再打電話來；或是你再打電話給某人。

好說好用 1

W: She cannot come to the phone now.
她現在不能來聽電話。

M: Okay.
好的。

W: Will you call again later?
你以後還會再打嗎？

M: You bet.
會的。

好說好用 2

M: That rude lady called again at work today.
那個沒禮貌的女人又打電話來了。

W: What did she want?
她要什麼？

M: Nothing.
沒什麼。

She just wanted to complain.
她只是想抱怨。

W: About what?
抱怨什麼？

M: She said that I wasn't helping her.
她說我沒幫她的忙。

W: How rude.
真沒禮貌。

好說好用 3

W: When should I call again?
我應該什麼時候再打？

M: Call again in a week to see if we've gotten any in stock.
一個星期以後再打，看看我們有沒有貨進來。

W: Will you hold one for me if it comes in?
如果貨進來，你可不可以幫我留一個？

M: Yes.
好的。

單字慣用語

☐ rude	[rud]	沒禮貌
☐ complain	[kəmˈplen]	抱怨
☐ stock	[ˈstɑk]	存貨
☐ hold	[hold]	v. 留著
☐ in stock		有存貨

23

Catch you later.
以後再聊。

易開竅　

　「Catch you later.」是用在彼此要離開時説的，表示「再見、以後再聊」。

好說好用 1

M: I'm leaving now.
我現在要走了。

W: Okay, catch you later.
好的，以後再聊。

M: Sounds good.
好的。

W: I'll see you at school.
我到學校再見你。

好說好用 2

W: Hey, I'll catch you later.
嗨，以後再聊。

M: Where are you going?
你要去哪裡？

W: I'm going home.
我要回家。

M: Oh.
噢。

好說好用 3

M: We've gotta go.
我們該走了。

We'll catch you later.
我們以後再跟你聊。

W: Let's meet for dinner.
我們一起吃晚飯。

M: Okay.
好的。

W: Meet us at 7:00.
七點等我們。

單字慣用語

☑ catch	['kætʃ]	趕上
☑ meet	['mit]	見面
☑ Sounds good.		聽起來是個好主意。

Come to see us again.
以後再來看我們。

 MP3-8

易開竅

「Come to see us again.」是一句用在訪客要離開時，主人向訪客說的話。

好說好用 1

W: It was so good seeing you again.
很高興再見到你們。

M: Yes, I enjoyed our visit.
是啊，我們這一次來訪我很愉快。

W: Me too.
我也是。

M: You'll have to come see us again.
你們以後還要再來看我們。

W: I plan to next Spring.
我計畫明年春天來。

M: Great, we'll be glad to have you.
很好，我們會很高興你們來。

好說好用 2

M: Thank you for shopping with us.
謝謝你陪我們上街購物。

W: Sure.
沒什麼。

M: Come back to see us again soon.
有空再來看我們。

W: I will.
我會的。

好說好用 3

W: Come back and see us again real soon.
儘快再回來看我們。

M: How late are you open?
你們開到多晚？

W: Until 9:00.
開到九點。

M: Great, see you soon.
好，再見。

單字慣用語

☑ enjoy	[ɪn′dʒɔɪ]	v. 喜歡
☑ visit	[′vɪzɪt]	拜訪
☑ shopping	[′ʃɑpɪŋ]	購物

Could I join you?
我可不可以加入？

易開竅   *MP3 -9*

　　若你想跟別人用同一張桌子，或是想加入別人的活動，你都可以用「Could I join you?」這句話來問。

好說好用 1

M: Excuse me, but could I join you?
對不起，我可以坐這裡嗎？

W: Sure, have a seat.
當然可以，請坐。

M: Thank you.
謝謝。

W: What is your name?
你叫什麼名字？

M: John.
約翰。

W: Hi, I'm Mary.
嗨，我叫瑪麗。

好說好用 2

W: May I please join you?
我可不可以加入？

M: Sure. Would you like a cup of coffee?
當然可以。你要不要喝一杯咖啡？

W: Yes, I would love one.
好的，我想喝一杯。

M: How do you take your coffee?
你要怎樣的咖啡？

好說好用 3

W: Could you join me for a drink after work?
下班後你要不要和我去喝一杯咖啡？

M: I would love to.
我很樂意。

W: Great, I'll see you then.
很好，到時候見。

M: All right.
好的。

單字慣用語

☑ join	[dʒɔɪn]	加入
☑ seat	[ˈsit]	座位
☑ have a seat		請坐
☑ after work		下班後
☑ all right		好的

Dear me!
糟了！

易開竅

「Dear me!」是一句帶有後悔或表示事情不好了的意思。

好說好用 1

W: Dear me!
糟了！

What time is it?
現在幾點了？

M: It's three o'clock.
三點。

W: Already?
已經三點了？

M: Yes, why?
是啊，怎麼啦？

W: I had a doctor's appointment at 2:30.
我跟醫生約好兩點半見他。

M: Um..., that's too bad.
嗯……那真糟糕。

好說好用 2

M: I spilled my milk.
我打翻了牛奶。

W: Oh, dear me!
噢，真不妙！

M: Help me clean it up.
幫我清理乾淨。

W: Okay.
好的。

好說好用 3

W: Dear me!
糟了！

I forgot to turn off the oven.
我忘了關火爐。

M: Oh, no.
噢，不好。

W: Will you do it for me?
你可以幫我關嗎？

M: I guess.
應該沒問題。

單字慣用語

☑ appointment [əˈpɔɪntmənt] 約會

☑ spilled [spɪld] 使溢出

☑	forgot	[fɚˈgɑt]	忘記（forget 的過去式）
☑	oven	[ˈʌvən]	火爐
☑	guess	[gɛs]	猜想
☑	clean up		清理乾淨
☑	turn off		關掉

MEMO

Do I make myself clear?
你真的聽懂我的話嗎？

易開竅

　　「Do I make myself clear?」這句話是用在「你禁止對方做什麼事，或是不答應對方做什麼事時，問對方真的聽得懂你說的話嗎」的時候。

好說好用 1

W: I want you to clean your room before you go out with your friends.
在你跟朋友出去之前，我要你把房間清理乾淨。

M: Okay.
好的。

W: Do I make myself clear?
你真的聽懂我的話嗎？

M: Yes.
是的。

好說好用 2

M: I do not want you to see him again.
我不要你再見他。

W: But, I really like him.
但是，我真的喜歡他。

M: Do I make myself clear?
我的話你聽懂了嗎？

W: I understand what you are saying.
我懂得你說的話。

But I'm going to see him anyway.
但是我還是要見他。

M: You're grounded.
你被禁足了。

W: You can't do that.
你不能這樣做。

好說好用 3

W: Am I making myself clear?
我的話你聽懂了嗎？

M: Yes, I understand.
是的，我聽得懂。

W: Do you understand what I'm trying to say?
你瞭解我想說的話嗎？

M: Yes, I understand.
是的，我瞭解。

單字慣用語

☑ clean	[klin]	v. 清理乾淨
☑ grounded	[ˈɡraʊndɪd]	被禁止做某事
☑ clear	[klɪr]	清楚
☑ understand	[ˌʌndɚˈstænd]	瞭解

Don't make me laugh.
別讓我笑了。

易開竅

　　當你認為對方所說的話太離譜了，你可以說「Don't make me laugh.」，這時對方就知道，你完全不贊同他所說的話。

好說好用 1

M: One day, I am going to be president.
　　有一天，我會做總統。

W: Ha, ha! Don't make me laugh.
　　哈，哈！別讓我笑了。

M: I might be.
　　我可能會做得到。

W: You'll never make it.
　　你永遠也做不到。

M: We'll see about that.
　　讓我們等著瞧。

W: Okay.
　　好的。

好說好用 2

W: Do you think you passed the test?
　　你想你有及格嗎？

M: Don't make me laugh.
別讓我笑了。

W: Why?
為什麼？

M: There is no way I passed that test.
那個考試我不可能及格的。

好說好用 3

M: I think she is really cute.
我認為她很漂亮。

W: Oh, don't make me laugh.
噢，別讓我笑了。

M: Why, don't you think she is cute?
為什麼，你不認為她漂亮嗎？

W: No, I don't.
不，我不認為她漂亮。

單字慣用語

☑ president	['prɛzɪdənt]	總統
☑ laugh	[læf]	笑
☑ passed	[pæst]	v.（考試）及格（pass 的過去式）
☑ cute	[kjut]	漂亮
☑ there is no way		不可能的

Don't speak too soon.
別說得太早。

當你認為事情還沒弄清楚前,不能太早下斷言,你可以告訴對方說「Don't speak too soon.」,也就是告訴對方,「你說的未必對」。

好說好用 1

W: I think I won the election.
我想這次選舉我贏了。

M: Careful, don't speak too soon.
小心點,別說得太早。

W: Why?
為什麼?

M: Because you never know how things will turn out.
因為你不會知道事情的結果會如何。

W: That's true.
那倒是真的。

M: Yes, but you probably did win.
是啊,但你可能真的贏了。

好說好用 2

M: The Cowboys have this game wrapped up.
這場比賽牛仔隊有充分的準備。

W: Don't speak too soon.
別說得太早。

M: Oh, they will win.
噢，他們會贏的。

W: You said that last week and they lost.
上星期你也這麼說，他們卻輸了。

好說好用 3

W: I may have spoken too soon last week.
上星期我可能說得太早了。

M: Why?
為什麼？

W: I said I could go with you and I can't.
我說我可以跟你一起去，但是我沒辦法去。

M: Oh, no.
噢，真不妙。

單字慣用語

☑ won	[wʌn]	贏（win 的過去式）
☑ election	[ɪˈlɛkʃən]	選舉
☑ probably	[ˈprɑbəblɪ]	可能
☑ win	[wɪn]	贏
☑ game	[gem]	比賽
☑ wrapped up something		有充分的準備
☑ lost	[lɔst]	v. 輸了（lose 的過去分詞）
☑ turn out		結果

Don't even think about it.
連想都別想。

  MP3-14

> 對方想做某件事，你認為那是不可能做成的，或是做了之後的效果肯定不好，為了要告訴他別做，甚至於「連想都別想」，英語就是「Don't even think about it.」。

好說好用 1

W: I might ask him out on a date.
我可能會約他出去。

M: Don't even think about it.
連想都別想。

W: Why?
為什麼？

M: Because he likes Mary.
因為他喜歡瑪麗。

W: So?
那又如何？

M: So, he only wants to go out with her.
那就是說，他只想要跟她出去。

好說好用 2

M: Don't even think about taking my car out for a spin.
別想要開我的車子出去兜風。

W: Aw, come on.
噢，別這樣。

M: Not a chance.
門都沒有。

W: Come on, I won't wreck it.
別這樣，我不會把它撞壞的。

好說好用 3

W: I'm thinking about cutting my hair.
我正在考慮要把頭髮剪短。

M: Don't even think about it.
連想都別想。

W: Why?
為什麼？

M: Because you wouldn't look good with short hair.
因為你剪短頭髮不會好看的。

單字慣用語

☑ spin	[spɪn]	急馳
☑ wreck	[rɛk]	撞壞（車子）
☑ ask someone out		約某人出去
☑ go out with...		跟某人出去
☑ come on		別這樣
☑ not a chance		門都沒有
☑ think about		考慮

14

Don't be too sure.
別太肯定。

易開竅 *MP3-15*

　　你認為對方説的未必是對的，你要叫他別説得那麼肯定，這時你可以對他説「Don't be too sure.」。

好說好用 1

M: I know I made an A on this test.
我知道這次的考試我拿到 A。

W: Don't be too sure.
別太肯定。

W: But, I am sure.
但是，我很確定。

M: We'll see.
等著瞧吧。

好說好用 2

W: I know Mary will win the contest.
我知道這次比賽瑪麗會贏。

M: You can't be too sure of these things.
這種事你不能太肯定的。

W: Why don't you think she'll win?
你為何認為她不會贏？

M: I don't know, the other girl is very good, too.
我不知道，另外那個女孩也很好。

W: Yes, but Mary is better.
是的，但是瑪麗比她更好。

M: I don't know about that.
這我可不知道。

好說好用 3

M: I think he is guilty.
我認為他有罪。

W: Don't be so sure.
別這麼肯定。

It could be someone else.
也可能是別人。

M: I guess we'll wait and see.
我想我們只好等著瞧。

W: I guess so.
好吧。

單字慣用語

☑	guilty	[ˈgɪltɪ]	有罪
☑	contest	[ˈkɑntɛst]	比賽
☑	better	[ˈbɛtɚ]	更好
☑	I guess so.		我想是吧。

Don't ask!
別問，我不想說！

易開竅

有時遇到很糟的事情，你不想再提起，而有人問你時，你可以說「Don't ask!」或是對方問你問題，你不願意把答案告訴對方時，你也可以說「Don't ask!」。

好說好用 1

W: How did your day go?
今天怎麼樣？

M: It was horrible.
很糟。

W: Why?
為什麼？

M: Don't ask.
別問。

W: What happened?
發生了什麼事？

M: Don't ask.
別問。

好說好用 2

M: How was the meeting?
會議開得怎麼樣？

W: Don't ask.
別問，我不想說。

M: That bad?
有那麼糟嗎？

W: Yes.
是的。

好說好用 3

W: How old are you?
你幾歲？

M: Don't ask.
別問。

W: You can't be over 30.
你不會超過三十歲啊。

M: Oh, yes I can.
噢，就是超過了。

單字慣用語

☑ horrible	[ˈhɔrəbl̩]	很糟
☑ bad	[bæd]	不好
☑ happened	[ˈhæpənd]	發生

Fine with me.
我沒有問題。

🔘 *MP3-17*

易開竅

大家在商量事情，或是有人問你某件事會不會打擾你，而你認為沒有問題，這時你可以說「Fine with me.」。

好說好用 1

W: Is pizza all right with you for dinner?
晚餐吃比薩餅，你有沒有問題？

M: Fine with me.
我沒問題。

W: What kind do you like?
你喜歡哪一種？

M: Extra cheese.
乳酪多一點的。

好說好用 2

M: Can I have a friend spend the night?
我可以讓朋友來過夜嗎？

W: I don't care.
我不在乎。

M: Are you sure?
你確定嗎？

W: Yes, it's fine with me.
是的，我沒問題。

M: What time can they come over?
他們什麼時候可以過來？

W: Anytime.
隨時都可以。

好說好用 3

W: Does it bother you if I smoke?
我抽煙會令你不舒服嗎？

M: No, it's fine with me.
不會，我沒問題。

W: Great.
好棒。

M: No problem.
沒問題的。

單字慣用語

☑ pizza	['pitsə]	比薩餅
☑ extra	['ɛkstrə]	多餘的
☑ cheese	[tʃiz]	乳酪
☑ bother	['bɑðɚ]	打擾
☑ smoke	[smok]	抽煙
☑ spend the night		過夜
☑ come over		過來

Go for it.
好好拼。

易開竅　　　　　　　　　　

「Go for it.」是一句勸對方為了目標好好努力的話。

好說好用 1

M: I am trying to make straight A's this semester.
這學期我正試著要拿全 A 的成績。

W: Go for it.
好好拼。

M: Do you think I can do it?
你認為我做得到嗎？

W: Yes, I'll help you.
做得到，我會幫忙你。

好說好用 2

W: Do you think I should try out for cheerleader next year?
你認為明年我應該參加啦啦隊的選拔嗎？

M: Go for it.
好好去拼。

W: Do you really think I should?
你真的認為我應該嗎？

M: Sure, you have nothing to lose.
是啊，你不會有任何損失。

W: Do you think I'm good enough?
你認為我夠好嗎？

M: Absolutely.
當然。

好說好用 3

M: I am not going to chicken out.
我不會臨陣退縮。
I'm going to go for it.
我會好好地拼。

W: Good for you.
有你的。

M: Will you help me?
你會幫忙我嗎？

W: Of course.
當然會。

單字慣用語

☑ straight	[stret]	連續的
☑ semester	[sə'mɛstɚ]	學期
☑ cheerleader	['tʃɪrlidɚ]	啦啦隊
☑ absolutely	['æbsə,lutlɪ]	肯定地
☑ chicken v	['tʃɪkən]	畏怯
☑ chicken out		臨陣退縮
☑ of course		當然

Have fun.
祝你玩得愉快。

易開窟 *MP3-19*

有人要去玩，或參加某種好玩的活動，你可以說「Have fun.」，祝對方玩得愉快。

好說好用 1

W: What are you doing this weekend?
這個週末你要做什麼？

M: I'm going skiing.
我要去滑雪。

W: Oh, well. Have fun.
噢，那，祝你玩得愉快。

M: I will.
我會的。

好說好用 2

M: Have fun tonight.
祝你今晚玩得愉快。

W: Thanks, you too.
謝謝你，也祝你今晚玩得愉快。

M: I hope you enjoy the show.
我希望你喜歡那個表演。

W: I'm sure I will.
我相信我會的。

好說好用 3

W: I hope you have fun at your party.
我希望你在你的宴會上玩得愉快。

M: We will.
我會的。

W: When will you be home?
你什麼時候回來？

M: Late.
很晚。

W: How late?
多晚？

M: After midnight.
午夜過後。

單字慣用語

☑ skiing	[ˈskiɪŋ]	滑雪
☑ show	[ʃo]	表演
☑ midnight	[ˈmɪdˌnaɪt]	午夜
☑ go skiing		去滑雪

How do you like that?
你喜不喜歡？

Unit 19

易 開 竅　　　　　　　　　　　　　🔘 *MP3-20*

「How do you like that?」這句話有幾種不同的意思，在本
單元是問對方對某件東西的意見。

好說好用 1

M: How do you like our new teacher?
你喜不喜歡我們的新老師？

W: She's okay.
她是不錯。

But I liked Mr. Lin better.
但是我較喜歡林先生。

M: Me, too.
我也是。

This lady is hard.
這位女士很嚴格。

W: I don't mind her being hard, as long as she is a good teacher.
只要她是個好老師，我不介意她嚴格。

好說好用 2

W: How do you like that new soft drink?
你喜不喜歡那個新冷飲？

M: I don't.
我不喜歡。

How do you like it?
你喜不喜歡？

W: I like it a lot.
我非常喜歡。

M: Gross.
好噁心。

好說好用 3

M: Hey, what's up?
嘿，有什麼事？

W: Nothing much.
沒什麼？

M: How do you like my new outfit?
你喜不喜歡我的新衣服？

W: It is very nice.
很好看。

M: Do you really think so?
你真的這麼認為嗎？

W: Yes, of course.
是的，當然囉。

單字慣用語

☑ hard	[hard]	嚴厲的
☑ mind	[maɪnd]	v. 介意
☑ drink	[drɪŋk]	飲料
☑ gross	[gros]	（食物）令人噁心的
☑ outfit	[ˈaʊtˌfɪt]	服裝
☑ as long as		只要
☑ of course		當然
☑ soft drink		冷飲

MEMO

How do you like that?

你會相信嗎？

易開罐

「How do you like that?」這句話在本單元是對某人的壞行為、奇怪的行為，或是對令人驚異的事件表示驚嘆。

好說好用 1

W: Well, how do you like that, they left without me.

噢，你會相信嗎，他們把我留下就走了。

M: What did they do that for?

他們為什麼這麼做？

W: Maybe they are mad at me.

或許他們在生我的氣。

M: I doubt it.

我不太相信。

好說好用 2

M: Your pants have a hole in them.

你的褲子有破洞。

W: Well, how do you like that?

噢，你會相信嗎？

M: You'd better get someone to sew them.

你最好找人把它縫補起來。

W: I will.
我會的。

好說好用 3

W: How do you like that?
你相信有這回事嗎？

M: What?
什麼事？

W: My teacher is on the news.
我們老師上報了。

M: Mr. Lin?
是林先生嗎？

W: Yes.
是的。

He stopped a burglary.
他逮到小偷。

M: How exciting!
多刺激啊！

單字慣用語

☐ burglary	[ˈbɝɡlərɪ]	偷竊
☐ exciting	[ɪkˈsaɪtɪŋ]	令人興奮的
☐ mad	[mæd]	生氣
☐ doubt	[daʊt]	懷疑

☑ pants	[pænts]	褲子
☑ hole	[hol]	洞
☑ sew	[so]	縫補
☑ be mad at...		生氣
☑ had better		最好

MEMO

How do you like that?
你喜歡那樣嗎？

易 開 竅 *MP3-22*

「How do you like that?」也可以用在處罰對方後，問對方喜歡被處罰的滋味嗎？

好說好用 1

W: Can I come out of my room yet?
我可以從我的房間出來了嗎？

M: You still have an hour to go.
你還有一個小時。

W: I said I was sorry.
我已經說過，我很抱歉。

M: Sorry doesn't cut it.
抱歉不能解決事情。

How do you like being locked up in there?
你喜歡被鎖在裡面嗎？

W: I don't.
我不喜歡。

M: Well, then remember that.
嗯，那就要記住。

好說好用 2

M: How did you like that?
你喜歡那樣嗎？

W: I didn't.
我不喜歡。

M: Well, then you should think about this the next time you are about to lie to me.
嗯，那麼下一次你想對我說謊的時候，就要好好地想一想。

W: I've learned my lesson.
我已經學到教訓了。

好說好用 3

W: How do you like that?
你喜歡那樣嗎？

M: I'm sorry.
我很抱歉。

W: Then don't ever be disrespectful again.
那麼就別再沒禮貌。

M: I won't.
我不會的。

I promise.
我向你保證。

單字慣用語

☐ disrespectful	[ˌdɪsrɪˈspɛktfəl]	沒禮貌
☐ promise	[ˈprɑmɪs]	保證
☐ lie	[laɪ]	説謊
☐ locked	[ˈlɑkt]	鎖（lock 的過去分詞）
☐ learn the lesson		學到教訓
☐ come out of		出來
☐ locked up		鎖起來

MEMO

22

How's it going?
你好嗎？

🔘 *MP3 -23*

「How's it going?」是向對方問好的說法之一。

好說好用 1

W: Hey, Tom, how's it going?
嗨，湯姆，你好嗎？

M: It's going great.
很好。

How about you?
哪你呢？

W: Things are going well.
一切都很好。

好說好用 2

M: Hi, how are you?
嗨，你好嗎？

W: Fine, how's it going?
很好，你呢？

M: Fine.
很好。

W: I hear you just graduated.
我聽說你剛畢業。

M: Yes, I did.
是的。

W: Congratulations!
恭喜！

單字慣用語

☐ graduated ['grædʒʊ,etɪd] 畢業

☐ congratulations [kən,grætʃə'leʃənz] 恭喜

MEMO

Unit 23

Is that so?
真的嗎？

易開竅 MP3 -24

「is that so?」是表示對於對方說的話，你帶點存疑的意思。

好說好用 1

M: Did you know that John and I have been best friends since kindergarten?
你知道約翰和我從幼稚園時，就是最好的朋友嗎？

W: Is that so?
真的嗎？

M: Yes, we do everything together.
是啊，我們每件事都一起做。

W: That's great.
那好棒。

好說好用 2

W: You look really good in red.
你穿紅色很好看。

M: Is that so?
真的嗎？

W: Yes, I think you should wear it more often.
真的，我認為你應該更常穿紅色。

M: I will
我會的。

好說好用 3

M: Is it so that you got an A on your exam?
你考試得了 A，是真的嗎？

W: Yes, it is so.
是的，是真的。

M: How did you manage that?
你如何做到的？

W: I studied hard.
我很認真讀。

M: So did I, but I got a B.
我也是，但是我只拿到 B。

W: Oh, better luck next time.
噢，希望你下一次運氣好一點。

單字慣用語

☑ kindergarten	[ˈkɪndɚˌgɑrtn̩]	幼稚園
☑ wear	[wɛr]	穿
☑ exam	[ɪgˈzæm]	考試
		（examination 的縮寫）
☑ manage	[ˈmænɪdʒ]	設法做到
☑ next time		下一次

Is that so?
24
我不相信！

易開窺

同樣是對對方説的話表示存疑，但是在説「Is that so?」時，「語調放平」，表示你不相信，這是有點不禮貌的説法，除了很熟的朋友，最好不要用！

好說好用 1

W: My parents bought me a car for my birthday.
我父母買了一部車給我做生日禮物。

M: Is that so?
我不相信！

W: Yes.
真的。

M: What does it look like?
是什麼樣的車子？

W: It is a red sports car.
是一部紅色的跑車。

M: Wow, I'm jealous.
哇，我真羨慕你。

好說好用 2

M: I'm almost positive I am getting a raise at work.
我確定我會得到加薪。

W: Is that so?
我不相信！

M: Yes, the boss told me he wants to talk to me.
真的，老闆告訴我他要跟我談談。

W: Maybe he is going to fire you.
或許他要把你解聘。

M: I don't think so.
不會的。

W: Whatever you say.
隨便你怎麼說。

好說好用 3

W: I found these shoes on sale for $500.
我在打折拍賣時，找到這雙鞋子，只賣五百元。

M: Is that so?
我不相信！

W: Yes, do you like them?
真的，你喜歡嗎？

M: Yes, where did you get them?
喜歡，你在哪裡買的？

W: At Far East department store.
在遠東百貨公司。

M: I'm going to get me some.
我要去買一些。

單字慣用語

☑ bought	[bɔt]	買（buy 的過去式）
☑ found	[faʊnd]	找到（find 的過去式）
☑ department	[dɪˈpɑrtmənt]	部門
☑ jealous	[ˈdʒɛləs]	嫉妒
☑ boss	[bɔs]	老闆
☑ fire	[ˈfaɪr]	v. 解雇
☑ department store		百貨公司
☑ sports car		跑車

MEMO

I don't believe this.
我真不相信竟有這種事。

Unit
25

易 開 竅

MP3-26

「I don't believe this.」是表示所發生的事太過離奇，令人難以相信。

好說好用 1

M: After the guy tripped me with his bag, he ran into my car in the parking lot.
那傢伙用袋子把我絆倒後，跑進我停在停車場的車子裡。

W: I don't believe this.
我真不相信竟有這種事。

M: I couldn't believe it, either.
我也不相信。

好說好用 2

W: I don't believe this.
我真不相信竟有這種事。

Are you telling me you two know each other?
你是在說你們兩個互相認識？

M: Yes, we met at summer camp when we were 10.
是的，我們十歲的時候在夏令營認識的。

67

W: I just don't believe this.
我真是不敢相信。

M: I know.
我知道。

It is weird.
這有點奇怪。

W: Did you ever keep in touch?
你們有保持聯繫嗎？

M: We used to write a long time ago.
很久以前我們有寫信。

好說好用 3

M: I am quitting my job.
我要辭職。

W: I don't believe this.
我真不相信竟有這種事。

M: Why?
為什麼？

W: You love your job.
你喜歡你的工作啊。

單字慣用語

☑ quitting	[ˈkwɪtɪŋ]	停止（quit 的現在分詞）
☑ tripped	[trɪpt]	絆倒（trip 的過去分詞）

☑ weird　　　　　[wɪrd]　　　　奇怪的

☑ parking lot　　　　　　　　　停車場

☑ summer camp　　　　　　　　夏令營

☑ keep in touch　　　　　　　　保持聯繫

MEMO

I am just looking.
我只是到處看看。

易開竅　　　　　　　　　　　　MP3-27

　　當你到店裡看東西時，若有店員過來問你時，你可以回答：「I am just looking.」，表示你只想先看看有什麼喜歡的。

好說好用 1

M: Can I help you with something, ma'am?
小姐，我可以幫你的忙嗎？

W: No, thank you.
不用，謝謝。

I am just looking.
我只是到處看看。

M: Are you looking for anything in particular?
你要找什麼東西嗎？

W: No, I am just looking.
沒有，我只是到處看看。

好說好用 2

W: Are you trying to find anything in particular?
你要找什麼東西嗎？

M: No, I am just looking.
沒有，我只是到處看看。

W: Let me know if I can be of assistance.
如果需要我幫忙的話，讓我知道。

M: Thank you, I will.
謝謝你，我會的。

好說好用 3

M: Do you need any help?
你需要幫忙嗎？

W: Not right now, I am just looking.
現在不需要，我只是到處看看。

M: What are you looking for?
你在找什麼？

W: I'm looking for a red skirt.
我在找一件紅色的襯衫。

M: Let me show you one.
讓我拿一件給你看。

W: Thank you.
謝謝你。

單字慣用語

☑ particular	[pɚˈtɪkjəlɚ]	特別的
☑ assistance	[əˈsɪstəns]	幫忙
☑ show	[ʃo]	v. 拿來給（某人）看
☑ look for		尋找

It's for you.
給你的。

易開竅

 MP3 -28

「It's for you.」可以用在告訴某人「是你的電話。」或是你要給對方某件東西時說的，意思是「給你的。」

好說好用 1

W: The phone is for you.
你的電話。

M: Who is it?
是誰？

W: I didn't ask.
我沒有問。

M: All right.
好吧。

好說好用 2

M: Hello. Just one second.
哈囉。請等一下。

W: Who is it for?
給誰的？

M: It's for you.
給你的。

W: Who is it?
是誰？

好說好用 **3**

W: What is this?
這是什麼？

M: It's for you.
給你的。

W: You got me a gift?
你買了一個禮物給我？

M: Yes.
是的。

W: Thank you.
謝謝你。

單字慣用語

☑ phone	[fon]	電話
☑ second	['sɛkənd]	（口語）片刻
☑ gift	[gɪft]	禮物
☑ just one second		等一下

Unit 28

It's on me.
我請客。

 MP3-29

易開竅

「請客」的動詞是「treat」，但也可以說「It's on me.」，表示「由我來付錢。」

好說好用 1

M: Do you want to go to a movie?
你要不要去看電影？

W: I don't know.
我不知道。

M: Oh, come on.
噢，別這樣。

It's on me.
我請客。

W: Okay.
好吧。

好說好用 2

W: Let's go out to lunch.
我們去吃午飯。

M: I can't.
我不能去。

I don't have any money.
我沒有錢。

W: That's okay, it's on me.
沒問題，我請客。

M: Well, in that case, okay.
嗯，那樣的話，好吧。

W: Great.
好。

M: Let's go.
走吧。

好說好用 3

M: Hey, dinner is on me.
嘿，晚飯我請客。

W: Why, did you inherit a lot of money?
為什麼，你繼承很多錢嗎？

M: No, I just want to treat you.
沒有，我只是想請你客。

W: Thanks.
謝謝你。

單字慣用語

☑ inherit	[ɪnˈhɛrɪt]	繼承
☑ treat	[trit]	v. 請客
☑ in that case		如果是那樣的話
☑ go to a movie		去看電影

Unit 29

I guess.
我猜想。

 MP3-30

「I guess.」是一句不太肯定的答話，也帶有猜測的意思。

好說好用 1

W: Can you pick Mary up after school today?
今天瑪麗放學時你可不可以去接她？

M: I guess.
應該可以。

W: Thank you, I appreciate it.
謝謝你，我很感激。

M: You're welcome.
不用客氣。

好說好用 2

M: Will you give me a hand next week at work?
下星期你可以幫忙我的工作嗎？

W: I guess.
應該可以。

M: You don't have to.
你並不是非做不可。

W: No, I will.
沒關係，我可以做。

M: Thank you.
謝謝你。

W: Okay.
好的。

好說好用 3

W: What time do you think they will get home?
你想他們何時會到家？

M: Around eight, I guess.
我想，大約在八點左右。

W: You mean you don't know for sure?
你是説你不太確定？

M: They didn't tell me.
他們沒告訴我。

單字慣用語

☐ appreciate	[ə′priʃɪ,et]	感激
☐ give me a hand		幫我一個忙
☐ pick up someone		接某人

Keep in touch.
保持聯繫。

易開窗 *MP3 -31*

> 「Keep in touch.」是一個片語，是「彼此保持聯繫」的意思。

好說好用 1

M: I'll send you my new address
我會寄我的新地址給你。

W: Good.
好的。

M: We need to keep in touch.
我們必須保持聯繫。

W: We will.
我們會的。

好說好用 2

W: Let's try to keep in touch.
我們要試著保持聯繫。

M: I promise to write.
我一定會寫信。

W: And I will call when I can.
有空我會打電話。

M: You'd better.
你最好要打。

W: I promise.
我會的。

好說好用 3

M: Do you still keep in touch with Mary?
你還有跟瑪麗保持聯繫嗎？

W: I did for a while, but I don't anymore.
我曾跟她保持聯繫一陣子，但現在沒有了。

M: What happened?
發生了什麼事？

W: I don't know, we just lost touch.
不知道，就是失去聯繫了。

單字慣用語

☐ address	[əˈdrɛs]	地址
☐ promise	[ˈprɑmɪs]	保證
☐ keep in touch with		跟某人保持聯絡
☐ lost touch		失去聯絡

Unit 31

Let it be.
順其自然吧。

易開竅　　　　　　　　　　　 MP3 -32

「Let it be.」是一句口語，表示「讓事情保持原狀，不要去管它，讓它順其自然」。

好說好用 1

W: What are you going to do about the argument?
這次的爭執你打算怎麼辦？

M: I'm just going to let it be.
我打算就順其自然。

W: Do you think it will blow over?
你認為事情會過去嗎？

M: Yes, I think it will.
是的，我認為會過去。

好說好用 2

M: Should I try to talk to him?
我應該試著跟他談談嗎？

W: No, just let him be.
不用，隨他去。

M: You're probably right.
你可能是對的。

W: I know I am.
我知道我是對的。

好說好用 3

M: I'm going to apologize to her.
我要去跟她道歉。

W: Aw, just let it be.
噢，隨它去。

M: No, we need to talk it over.
不行，我們需要把事情談開。

W: I think you're wrong.
我認為你是錯的。

M: Well, I don't.
嗯，我沒有錯。

W: Whatever you say.
隨便你怎麼說。

單字慣用語

☑ argument	[ˈɑrgjəmənt]	爭執
☑ apologize	[əˈpɑlədʒaɪz]	道歉
☑ talk it over		討論它
☑ blow over		消失；過去

81

Ladies first.
女士優先。

MP3-33

　　這是一句男士要讓女士先走時說的話，通常用在進入電梯、進入房間或是在必須有前後次序進出時。若你是男士，要讓女士先走，只要說「Ladies first.」，該女士就會知道你要讓她。

好說好用 1

W: After you.
你先走。

M: No, after you — ladies first.
不，你先走—女士優先。

W: You are such a gentleman.
你真有紳士風度。

M: Thank you.
謝謝你。

好說好用 2

W: Do you want this seat?
你要這個座位嗎？

M: No, ladies first.
不，女士優先。

W: Well, if you insist.
嗯，如果你堅持的話。

M: Go ahead.
請吧。

好說好用 **3**

M: Ladies first.
女士優先。

W: You just don't want to be the first one to go.
你只是不想第一個走。

M: You're right.
你說對了。

W: Okay, I go in first.
好吧，我先進去。

單字慣用語

☐ insist　　　　　　　　[ɪnˈsɪst]　　　堅持

33 **Make no mistake.**
別弄錯。

MP3-34

易開竅

　　提醒對方別把事情弄錯了，說法就是「Make no mistake.」。

好說好用 1

W: Make no mistake, this is my jacket.
別弄錯，這是我的夾克。

M: But, it looks just like mine.
但是，它看起來跟我的一樣。

W: Yes, but it has my name in it.
是的，但是它有我的名字在上面。

M: Where?
在哪裡？

W: On the collar.
在領子上。

M: Oh, I see.
噢，我知道了。

好說好用 2

M: Will you save my seat for me?
你可以幫我留著我的座位嗎？

W: You are coming back then?
那麼你是會回來囉？

M: Yes, it may take me a while.
是的，我可能要一段時間。

But make no mistake, I will be back.
但是別弄錯，我會回來的。

W: All right.
好的。

好說好用 3

W: I will make no mistake about this.
這件事我不會弄錯的。

M: I'm glad to hear that.
我很高興聽到。

W: You can count on me.
你可以信得過我。

M: I hope so.
但願如此。

單字慣用語

☑ jacket	[ˈdʒækɪt]	夾克
☑ collar	[ˈkɑlɚ]	領子

Make it two.

我也要點同樣的。

Unit 34

 MP3-35

當你和同伴在點餐時，在同伴點完之後，你也想要跟對方點相同的東西，你只要對服務生說「Make it tow.」就可以了。

好說好用 1

M: Bartender, I'll have a margarita.
酒保，我要一杯瑪格麗特雞尾酒。

W: Make it two.
我也要同樣的。

M: Since when do you like margaritas?
你什麼時候開始喜歡瑪格麗特雞尾酒的？

W: I just wanted to try one.
我只是想試試看。

好說好用 2

W: For dinner, I will have the fried chicken and a salad.
晚餐，我要炸雞和沙拉。

M: That sounds good, make it two.
聽起來不錯，我也要同樣的。

W: Why do you always order the same thing I do?
你為什麼總是跟我點一樣的東西？

M: Because you always order the best things.
因為你點的總是最好的。

W: That's true.
那是事實。

M: I know.
我知道。

好說好用 3

M: Will you make that two steaks instead of one?
你可以把兩人份的牛排做成一人份的嗎？

W: Yes, sir.
好的，先生。

M: We'd like them cooked medium.
我要七分熟的。

W: Very well, sir.
好的，先生。

單字慣用語

☑ bartender	['bɑr,tɛndɚ]	酒保
☑ margarita	[,mɑrgə'ritə]	瑪格麗特雞尾酒
☑ steak	[stek]	牛排
☑ medium	['midɪəm]	七分熟

Make up your mind.
做個決定。

易開竅 🔘 *MP3-36*

「Make up your mind.」是一句成語，意思是叫對方做個決定。

好說好用 1

M: Are you coming or not?
你到底要不要來？

W: I haven't decided yet.
我還沒有決定。

M: Well, make up your mind.
那，做個決定吧。

W: Can I call you later?
我再打電話給你好嗎？

M: Okay, but don't take too long.
好吧，但不要太久。

好說好用 2

W: Which job do you think I should take?
你認為我該接哪個工作？

M: I wish you would just make up your mind.
我希望你能夠做個決定。

W: Well, both jobs have some very good features.
嗯，兩個工作都各有優點。

M: I know.
我知道。

It's such a difficult decision.
這很難做決定。

W: I just don't know what to do.
我就是不知道該怎麼辦。

M: Well, what job do you think would be more fun?
嗯，你認為哪個工作較有趣？

好說好用 3

M: I wish you would just make up your mind.
我希望你能夠做個決定。

W: What do you think I should wear?
你認為我該穿哪一件？

M: Well, if I were you, I would wear the pink dress.
嗯，如果我是你的話，我會穿粉紅色的洋裝。

W: Thanks.
謝謝你。

單字慣用語

☑	decide	[dɪˈsaɪd]	決定
☑	feature	[ˈfitʃɚ]	特點
☑	difficult	[ˈdɪfəkəlt]	困難的
☑	decision	[dɪˈsɪʒən]	決定
☑	wear	[wɛr]	穿

MEMO

My point is...

我的重點是……

易開竅

說話有時說了許多，但是要說的重點其實很簡單，要告訴對方你說的重點是什麼，英語的說法就是「My point is...」。

好說好用 1

M: So, what is your point?
那麼，你要說的重點是什麼？

W: My point is that you're wasting your time at that job.
我要說的就是你做那個工作是在浪費時間。

M: But, I like my job.
但是，我喜歡我的工作。

W: You're missing the point.
你錯過我說的重點。

M: No, I'm not.
不，我沒有。

W: Yes, you are.
有的，你有。

好說好用 2

W: My point about all of this is that you need to be more responsible.
關於這整個，我說的重點是，你需要負責一點。

M: I am responsible.
我是很負責。

W: Don't make me laugh.
別讓我笑了。

M: I'm serious.
我是說真的。

好說好用 3

M: What is the point to all of this?
這整個的重點是什麼？

W: My point is that I want to help you.
我的重點就是我要幫你的忙。

M: Then leave me alone.
那麼就別管我。

W: Fine.
好的。

單字慣用語

☑ responsible	[rɪˈspɑnsəbl̩]	負責的
☑ serious	[ˈsɪrɪəs]	認真的，不是開玩笑的
☑ miss	[mɪs]	錯過
☑ point	[pɔɪnt]	重點

Not bad.
37
不錯。

易 開 竅

🔘 *MP3-38*

「Not bad.」是說某人或某件事是令人滿意的。

好說好用 1

W: How do like my new hair color?
你喜歡我的頭髮的新顏色嗎？

M: Not bad, but I liked you the way you were.
不錯，但是我喜歡你以前的樣子。

W: You did?
真的？

M: Yes.
是的。

好說好用 2

M: What do you say about this movie?
這部電影你認為怎麼樣？

W: Not bad, for an action film.
以動作片來說是很不錯。

M: Don't you like action films?
你不喜歡動作片嗎？

W: I like comedies better.
我較喜歡喜劇片。

M: Why didn't you say so before?
你先前怎麼沒説？

W: I didn't want to change your plans.
我不想改變你的計畫。

好說好用 3

W: Do you like my story?
你喜歡我的故事嗎？

M: Not bad, but you can do better.
不錯，但是你可以做得更好。

W: How?
怎麼做？

M: Write what you feel.
把你的感覺寫出來。

單字慣用語

☑ action film		動作片
☑ plan	[plæn]	計畫

Never mind.
算了。

易開竅

「Never mind.」意思是「算了。」表示沒什麼重要，就讓它過去算了。當你要告訴別人什麼事，或要別人幫你做什麼事，但他沒聽清楚，你覺得不做也沒關係時，就可以說「Never mind.」。

好說好用 1

M: Will you bring me a towel?
你可以拿一條毛巾給我嗎？

W: What did you say?
你說什麼？

M: Never mind.
算了。

W: Okay.
那好。

好說好用 2

W: Do you still want me to buy some milk?
你仍然要我買些牛奶嗎？

M: No, never mind.
不，不用了。

W: Did you already get some?
你已買了嗎？

M: Yes, I got some earlier.
是的，我稍早前買了。

好說好用 3

M: What were you going to tell me earlier?
你稍早前要跟我説什麼？

W: Never mind, it wasn't important.
算了，並不重要。

M: Oh, come on, tell me.
噢，別這樣，告訴我吧。

W: No, just never mind.
不，就算了。

單字慣用語

☑ towel	[taʊl]	毛巾
☑ important	[ɪmˈpɔrtənt]	重要的
☑ mind	[maɪnd]	介意

No sweat.

39

沒問題。

易 開 竅

🔘 *MP3-40*

　「No sweat.」表示「沒問題。」和「No problem.」的用法、意思一樣。

好說好用 1

M: I forgot to take out the trash.
我忘了把垃圾拿出去。

W: No sweat, I'll do it.
沒問題，我來做。

M: I really appreciate it.
我真的很感激。

W: Sure and you can do the dishes for me.
哪裡，那你可以幫我洗碗。

M: It's a deal.
就這麼說定。

W: Good.
好的。

好說好用 2

W: I think I made a mistake at work.
我想我在工作上犯了一個錯誤。

M: That's no sweat.
那也沒什麼。

W: Why do you say that?
你為什麼做麼説？

M: Because the boss loves you.
因為老闆喜歡你。

好說好用 3

M: Do you think you'll pass this test?
你認為這次考試你會及格嗎？

W: Sure. No sweat.
當然，沒問題的。

M: I hope you're right.
我希望你是對的。

W: I know I am.
我知道我是對的。

單字慣用語

☑ sweat	[swɛt]	流汗
☑ trash	[træʃ]	垃圾
☑ do the dishes		洗碗

No problem.
沒問題。

易開竅

「No problem.」是有人請你幫忙時，你答應時的說法，和「No sweat.」的用法一樣。

好說好用 1

W: Can you cover for me at work?
你可以代我的班嗎？

M: Sure, no problem.
當然可以，沒問題。

W: My shift is from 6:00-10:00.
我的班是六點到十點。

M: Oh, I can't do it then.
噢，那個時間我不能做。

好說好用 2

M: I want to thank you for helping me.
我要謝謝你幫我的忙。

W: It was no problem.
那沒什麼。

M: How can I repay you?
我該如何報答你？

W: There is no need to.
不需要。

M: But I want to.
但是我想要。

W: Then buy me dinner some time.
那麼有空請我吃晚餐。

好說好用 3

W: Can you pick the kids up after school?
你可以在小孩放學後去接他們嗎？

M: Sure, that's no problem.
當然可以，沒問題。

W: Great. Thank you.
很好，謝謝你。

M: No problem.
沒什麼。

單字慣用語

☑ cover for		替人代班
☑ shift	[ʃɪft]	（班次）工作時間
☑ repay	[rɪˈpe]	報答

Now what?

現在要做什麼？

MP3-42

易開竅

「Now what?」就是事情都做完了，問看看接下來有什麼事要做。

好說好用 1

M: I finished raking the leaves.
我把草耙完了。

W: Great!
很好。

M: Now what?
現在要做什麼？

W: Bag them.
用袋子裝起來。

M: Do I have to?
我一定要做嗎？

W: Yes.
是的。

好說好用 2

W: Now what?
現在要做什麼？

M: I don't know.
我不知道。

W: Do you want to see a movie?
你要看電影嗎？

M: Anything you say.
隨便你。

好說好用 3

M: We already done all of that stuff.
那些事情我們都已經做完了。

W: So, now what?
那麼，現在要做什麼呢？

M: Do you have any ideas?
你有什麼主意嗎？

W: Yeah, let's go shopping.
有，我們去逛街。

單字慣用語

☑ raking	[ˈrekɪŋ]	耙（草）
		（rake 的動名詞）
☑ bag	[bæg]	v. 用袋子裝
☑ stuff	[stʌf]	事情
☑ go shopping		上街購物

Oh, yeah?
噢，是嗎？

易開竅 *MP3-43*

「Oh, yeah?」是表示對對方說的話很不以為然，有點不禮貌而且帶有挑戰意味。

好說好用 1

W: I can ride my bicycle faster than you.
我可以騎腳踏車騎得比你快。

M: Oh, yeah?
噢，是嗎？

W: Watch me.
你看著。

M: Go ahead, make my day.
做吧，好讓我不愉快。

W: I will.
我會的。

M: I'm waiting.
我在等著。

好說好用 2

M: I told you not to do that.
我跟你說過別做的。

W: So?
那又怎樣？

M: So, I was right.
我說對了。

W: Oh, yeah?
噢，是嗎？

M: Yeah.
是的。

W: We'll see about that.
我們等著瞧。

M: Give it up, I am right.
投降吧，我是對的。

W: No, you're not.
不，你不是。

好說好用 3

M: I'm going to have the most Christmas gifts.
我將有最多聖誕禮物。

W: Oh yeah?
噢，是嗎？

M: Yeah.
是的。

W: We'll see.
　　我們等著瞧。

單字慣用語

☑ ride	[raɪd]	騎（腳踏車）
☑ bicycle	[ˈbaɪˌsɪkl̩]	腳踏車
☑ faster	[ˈfæstɚ]	更快
		（fast 的比較級）

MEMO

Once and for all...

43

最後（終於）……

易開竅

MP3 -44

「Once and for all.」是指不管事情原本如何，到最後還是有不同的作法。

好說好用 1

M: Once and for all, I did not cheat on the test.
我考試終於沒有作弊。

W. I don't believe you.
我不相信。

M: That's not my problem.
那不是我的問題。

W: Whatever you say.
隨便你怎麼說。

好說好用 2

W: So, tell me again why you did it.
那，再跟我說一次你為什麼這麼做。

M: Once and for all, I wanted to prove I could.
我終究想證明我能做。

W: So you climbed a mountain?
所以你就去爬山？

M: Yes.
是的。

W: Were you scared?
你害怕嗎？

M: Not really.
不太怕。

好說好用 3

M: What are you saying?
你說什麼？

W: Once and for all, I am saying that I was wrong.
我終於說我錯了。

M: Is this an apology?
這是在道歉嗎？

W: Yes.
是的。

單字慣用語

☑ cheat	[tʃit]	（考試）作弊
☑ apology	[əˈpɑlədʒɪ]	道歉
☑ climbed	[klaɪmd]	爬（climb 的過去式）
☑ mountain	[ˈmaʊntn̩]	山

Please.
拜託。

Unit **44**

易 開 竅   ● *MP3 -45*

需要對方的幫忙時，加一聲「please」準沒錯，這是表示禮貌。或者當對方拒絕你的要求，或是對方對你提出的要求猶豫不決時，你對對方說聲「**Please.**」，也就是中文所說的「拜託」的意思。

好說好用 1

M: May I please stay up late?
我可以晚一點睡嗎？

W: I don't know.
我不知道。

M: Please.
拜託。

W: Well, all right.
嗯，好吧。

好說好用 2

W: Will you get me a piece of cake?
你可以幫我拿塊蛋糕嗎？

M: What do you say?
你應該說什麼？

W: Please.
拜託。

M: Okay.
好的。

好說好用 3

M: Please clean up your room.
請把你的房間整理乾淨。

W: I will.
我會的。

M: When?
什麼時候？

W: When I have time.
等我有空時。

M: That's not good enough — do it now.
那不行—現在就做。

W: I can't.
沒辦法。

單字慣用語

☑ stay up 熬夜

☑ clean up 清理乾淨

Oh, please.
噢，得了吧。

MP3 -46

「Oh, please.」是用在你不相信對方說的話，意思就是「噢，得了吧。」表示請他別信口開河。

好說好用 1

W: I've made straight A's this year.
今年我拿到全 A 的成績。

M: Oh, please, everybody knows you flunked math.
噢，得了吧。大家都知道你的數學不及格。

W: I did not.
我沒有。

M: Oh, please. Don't insult me.
噢，得了吧。別侮辱我的智慧。

W: I'm not, I really made an A.
我沒有，我真的得到全 A 的成績。

M: Yeah, right.
天相信。

好說好用 2

M: You hurt my feelings.
你傷了我的心。

W: Oh please, you know I wasn't serious.
噢，得了吧。你知道我不是説真的。

M: You seemed serious.
你看起來是説真的。

W: Well, I wasn't.
那，我不是的。

好說好用 3

W: I've been well behaved today.
我今天很守規矩。

M: Oh, please — you made your sister cry.
噢，得了吧—你把你的妹妹弄哭了。

W: She deserved it.
她應得的。

M: She did not.
那不是她應得的。

單字慣用語

☑ straight	[stret]	連續的
☑ flunked	[flʌŋkt]	（成績）不及格（flunk 的過去式）
☑ deserve	[dɪˈzɝv]	應受（懲罰或獎賞）
☑ well-behaved		很守規矩（well-behave 的過去式）

Shame on you.
你真丟臉。

易 開 竅

🔘 *MP3 -47*

有人做錯了事，你跟他說「Shame on you.」，讓他知道他做錯事了。

好說好用 1

W: Shame on you.
你真丟臉。

M: For what?
為了什麼事？

W: You weren't very nice to that girl.
你對待那個女孩的態度很不好。

M: That's because I don't like her.
那是因為我不喜歡她。

W: But, you don't have to be mean to her.
但是，你也不需要對她那麼刻薄。

M: Who cares?
管它的。

好說好用 2

M: Shame on you.
你真丟臉。

You know better than that.
你知道你該怎麼做的。

W: I know, I'll pick my coat up off the floor.
我知道，我會把地板上的外套撿起來。

M: Thank you.
謝謝你。

W: No problem.
沒問題。

好說好用 3

W: I am so upset with you.
我對你很生氣。

M: I did not do anything wrong.
我又沒做錯事。

W: Shame on you for the way you acted tonight.
你今晚的行為很丟臉。

M: I didn't mean to upset you.
我不是故意惹你生氣的。

單字慣用語

☑ shame	[ʃem]	羞恥；丟臉
☑ mean	[min]	a. 刻薄的
☑ mean	[min]	v. 意欲
☑ upset	[ʌpˈsɛt]	使不高興

Same to you.
我希望你也是。

易開竅

MP3-48

當有人告訴你「我希望你會如何」時，不管對方的希望是好事情或壞事情，如果你也希望對方得到相同的結果，就說「Same to you.」。

好說好用 1

M: I hope you have a good day.
我希望你玩得愉快。

W: Thanks, same to you.
謝謝你，我希望你也玩得愉快。

M: Thank you
謝謝你。

W: You're welcome.
不客氣。

好說好用 2

W: Good luck on your test.
祝你考試時有好運氣。

M: Same to you.
我希望你也一樣。

W: Thank you, I need it.
謝謝你，我需要好運氣。

M: No, you don't, you'll do fine.
不，你不需要的，你會考得很好。

W: Do you think so?
你這麼認為嗎？

M: Sure, you've really studied hard.
當然，你真的很用功。

好說好用 3

M: I hope you get grounded.
我希望你被禁足。

W: Same to you.
我希望你也一樣。

M: I didn't do anything wrong.
我並沒有做錯什麼事。

W: Neither did I.
我也沒有。

單字慣用語

| ☐ at least | 至少 |
| ☐ get grounded | 被罰不准做 |

48

So do I.
我也是。

🔘 *MP3 -49*

易 開 竅

對方告訴你一件事，而你要告訴他「我也一樣有」，若對方的句子裡用的是「一般動詞」，你要說「So do I.」；若對方的句子裡用的是「be 動詞」，你就要說「So am I.」。

好說好用 1

W: I go swimming every day after school.
我每天放學後去游泳。

M: So do I.
我也是。

W: Then how come I've never seen you at the pool?
那，為什麼我從沒在池邊看到你？

M: We must not go to the same pool.
我們一定去不同的游泳池。

好說好用 2

M: I am going on vacation soon.
我很快就要去度假。

W: So am I.
我也是。

M: Oh, please.
噢，得了吧。

You're not going anywhere.
你不會去任何地方的。

W: I am so.
我會去的。

好說好用 3

W: I have a cat.
我有一隻貓。

M: So do I.
我也是。

W: What color is it?
是什麼顏色的？

M: White.
白色的。

單字慣用語

| ☐ pool | [pul] | 游泳池 |
| ☐ vacation | [veˈkeʃən] | 度假 |

Stay out of this.
別管這件事。

告訴別人，這沒你的事，不要去介入，英文的說法就是「Stay out of this.」。

好說好用 1

M: He could have stopped the accident before it happened.
在車禍發生之前，他原本可以阻止它發生的。

W: You just stay out of this.
你別管這件事。

M: Why?
為什麼？

W: Because it is none of your business.
因為那沒你的事。

好說好用 2

W: Stay out of this.
別管這件事。

M: No, it affects me too.
不行，它也影響到我。

W: No, it doesn't.
不，它沒有影響到你。

M: Yes, it does.
有的，它影響到我。

好說好用 3

M: What did he say when you tried to tell him?
你試著告訴他時，他怎麼說？

W: He said "stay out of it".
他說「別管這件事」。

M: That was rude.
那真沒禮貌。

W: I thought so.
我也這麼想。

M: Maybe I should talk to him.
或許我該跟他談。

W: It won't do any good.
沒有用的。

單字慣用語

☐ accident	[ˈæksɪdənt]	車禍
☐ affect	[əˈfɛkt]	影響到
☐ rude	[rud]	沒禮貌
☐ none of your business		沒有你的事

Take it easy.
再見，要珍重。

易開竅 *MP3-51*

雙方要道別時，除了説「Good-bye」之外，也可以説「Take it easy.」，請對方凡事要小心，也就是要對方珍重。這也是道別時的説法之一。

好說好用 1

M: Goodnight. Take it easy.
晚安，多珍重。

W: You too.
你也是。

M: I'll call you tomorrow.
我明天打電話給你。

W: Okay.
好的。

好說好用 2

W: Thanks for inviting us.
謝謝你邀請我們。

M: We are glad you came.
我們很高興你們來。

W: Yes, it was good to see you.
是的，見到你們真好。

M: You take it easy, now.
要多珍重。

W: You, too.
你們也是。

M: We will.
我們會的。

好說好用 3

M: Take it easy and we'll see you tomorrow.
多珍重，明天見。

W: Okay. Good-bye.
好的，再見。

M: Good-bye.
再見。

W: See ya.
再見。

單字慣用語

☑ inviting　　　　　[ɪnˈvaɪtɪŋ]　　邀請

（invite 的動名詞）

☑ glad　　　　　　[glæd]　　　高興

Take it easy.
放輕鬆點。

易開竅　　　　　　　　　　　　　🔵 *MP3 -52*

「Take it easy.」除了用在道別時，也可用在說「要放輕鬆、別緊張」。

好說好用 1

M: What are you doing this weekend?
這個週末你要做什麼？

W: I think I'm just going to take it easy and relax.
我想我會放輕鬆，休息一下。

M: That sounds like a good idea.
那聽起來是個好主意。

W: Yes, I think I'll go to the movies.
是的，我想我會去看電影。

M: Good for you.
太好了。

W: Would you like to go with me?
你要不要跟我一起去？

好說好用 2

W: What you need to do is just take it easy for a while.
你需要做的就是放輕鬆一段時間。

M: You're right, but for how long?
你說得沒錯，但要多久？

W: At least until you get over this cold.
至少等到你的感冒好了。

M: Okay.
好的。

好說好用 3

M: The doctor told me to take it easy this week.
醫生要我這個星期放輕鬆一點。

W: That's good advice.
那是個好建議。

M: Is that so?
是嗎？

W: Yes, you have been doing too much lately.
是的，你最近做得太多了。

單字慣用語

☑ relax	[rɪˈlæks]	放鬆
☑ while	[hwaɪl]	一段時間
☑ advice	[ədˈvaɪs]	建議
☑ cold	[kold]	n. 感冒

Too bad.

那真糟。

52

易開竅

有人跟你說一件不幸的消息，你可以說「Too bad.」，表示你的同情。

好說好用 1

M: Mary broke her ankle.
瑪麗的腳踝受了傷。

W: Oh no, that's too bad.
噢，那真是糟。

M: Yeah, now she can't try out for cheerleader.
是啊，現在她不能參加啦啦隊隊長的選拔了。

W: That's horrible.
那真慘。

好說好用 2

W: It's really too bad that you can't go with us.
你不能跟我們去真是糟糕。

M: I know, I really wanted to.
我知道，我真的很想去。

W: Maybe next time.
或許下一次。

M: Please invite me again.
請再邀請我。

W: We will.
我們會的。

M: Good.
好。

好說好用 3

M: My brother is sick.
我弟弟病了。

W: That's too bad.
那真糟。

M: I had to take him to the doctor.
我必須帶他去看醫生。

W: Did he have to get a shot?
他必須要打針嗎？

單字慣用語

☑ ankle	[ˈæŋkl̩]	腳踝
☑ try out		選拔賽
☑ cheerleader	[ˈtʃɪrlidɚ]	啦啦隊隊長
☑ horrible	[ˈhɔrəbl̩]	（口語）糟透的
☑ shot	[ʃɑt]	注射

Too bad.
活該。（那也沒辦法。）

易 開 竅 *MP3 -54*

「Too bad.」也可以用在對別人的不幸事件，抱有幸災樂禍的意味，依說這句話者的語氣而定。

好說好用 1

M: That mean girl in class fell and got hurt.
班上那個刻薄的女孩跌倒受傷了。

W: Aw, that's too bad.
噢，活該。

M: Yeah, I'm really upset.
是啊，我真的很生氣。

W: Oh yeah, me too.
是嘛，我也是。

好說好用 2

W: I think I hurt his feelings.
我想我傷了他的心。

M: That's just too bad, he deserved it.
活該，他應得的。

W: I know, but I still feel bad.
我知道，但是我仍然很難過。

M: Don't, he would do the same to you.
別難過，他也會這樣對你的。

W: I know.
我知道。

M: So don't feel guilty.
所以別有罪惡感。

好說好用 3

M: My teacher gave me too much homework.
我們老師給我們太多功課了。

W: Aw, that's too bad.
噢，好慘哦。

M: Now, I won't have any free-time tonight.
喏，我今晚沒有自由的時間了。

W: Too bad.
那也沒辦法。

單字慣用語

☑ mean   [min]   a. 刻薄的

☑ fell   [fɛl]   v. 跌倒（fall 的過去式）

☑ guilty   [ˈgɪltɪ]   內疚的

That's too much.
那不行。（那太過分了。）

易開竅

要表示事情超過了可以接受的程度時，可以說「That's too much.」。

好說好用 1

W: My boss offered me a promotion and a raise.
我的老闆要給我晉級並加薪。

M: Oh, that's too much.
噢，那太過分了。

W: Yes, I am excited.
是啊，我好興奮。

M: When do you start your new job?
你什麼時候開始新工作？

W: A week from tomorrow.
明天算起一個星期。

M: Congratulations.
恭喜。

好說好用 2

M: When you finish with your plate, I will do the dishes.
你的盤子用完後，我要洗碗。

W: But you did the cooking.
但是你煮飯的。

M: So?
那又怎樣？

W: That's too much, I'll do the dishes.
那不行，我來洗碗。

好說好用 3

W: I just don't believe your story, that's too much.
我就是不相信你的故事，那太離譜了。

M: Yes, but it's true.
是的，但它是真的。

W: Can you prove it?
你能證明嗎？

M: Yes, I can.
是的，我能。

單字慣用語

☑ offer	[ˈɔfɚ]	提供
☑ boss	[bɔs]	老闆
☑ promotion	[prəˈmoʃən]	晉級
☑ excited	[ɪkˈsaɪtɪd]	興奮的
☑ raise	[rez]	加薪
☑ prove	[pruv]	證明
☑ plate	[plet]	盤子

Unit 55

This is it.
這就是了。

MP3-56

易開竅

在談話中，說到了你認為是關鍵的話，你可以說「This is it.」，表示「這就是我們需要搞清楚的重點」，或是「這就是我們在等待的」。

好說好用 1

W: Are you going with us to the movie?
你要跟我們去看電影嗎？

M: I don't know yet.
我還不知道。

W: This is it.
這就是了。

We need your decision.
我們需要你做決定。

M: Okay, I'll go.
好的，我會去。

W: Good, be ready by 6:00 p.m.
好，六點以前準備好。

M: Okay.
好的。

好說好用 2

W: I can't believe we are finally graduating.
我真不相信我們終於要畢業了。

M: Yes, this is it.
是啊，這就是了。

W: Now what?
那現在要怎樣？

M: I don't know.
我不知道。

好說好用 3

M: This is it, the final show of the evening.
這就是了，今晚最後的表演。

W: Yes, this is it.
是啊，這就是了。

M: I'm ready to go home now.
我已準備好要回家了。

W: Me too.
我也是。

單字慣用語

☑ graduating　　[ˈɡrædʒʊˌetɪŋ]　　畢業（graduate 的現在分詞）

☑ final　　[ˈfaɪnl]　　最後的

That does it.
我受夠了。

 MP3 -57

易開竅

　　「That does it.」有幾種不同的意思，在本單元是用來說「某件事太過分了，你已經忍無可忍了」。

好說好用 1

W: I can't stand you.
我真的受不了你。

M: That does it, get out of my house.
我受夠了，離開我的房子。

W: I'm leaving.
我正要離開。

M: Good.
好。

好說好用 2

M: That does it.
我受夠了。

W: What?
什麼？

M: I've had it up here with his loud stereo.
我已受不了他的音響開那麼大聲。

W: Tell him to turn it down.
告訴他開小聲一點。

M: I did, but he couldn't hear me.
我已經告訴他了，但是他聽不到。

W: I'll go talk to him.
我去告訴他。

好說好用 3

W: That does it, I give up.
我受夠了，我放棄。

M: Don't give up now.
不要現在放棄。

W: Why not?
為什麼不要？

M: Because you are so close to finishing.
因為你已快做到。

單字慣用語

☑ stand	[ˈstænd]	忍受
☑ stereo	[ˈstɛrɪo]	立體音響
☑ turn it down		轉小聲一點
☑ give up		放棄

That does it.
做好了。

MP3-58

易開竅

在本單元中，「That does it.」和上一個單元的意思不同，
表示「事情做好了」。

好說好用 1

W: Well, that does it.
嗯，做好了。

M: Is dinner ready?
晚餐好了嗎？

W: Yes.
是的。

M: I'll be right there.
我馬上來。

好說好用 2

M: Are you almost done?
你快做好了嗎？

W: Yes, that does it.
是的，做好了。

M: Great, let's test it out.
好的，讓我們來做測試。

W: Okay.
好的。

好說好用 3

W: Here's the last screw.
這是最後一個螺絲釘。

M: Great, that does it.
很好，做好了。

W: Will it work now?
現在可以用了嗎？

M: It should.
應該可以。

W: Let's try it out.
讓我們來試試看。

M: Okay.
好的。

單字慣用語

☑ last	[læst]	最後的
☑ screw	[skru]	螺絲釘
☑ try out		試試看

That's easy for you to say.
你說得倒輕鬆。

MP3-59

易開竅

當某件事對某人來說是很簡單或沒什麼影響，但對別人來說卻不一樣時，你可以告訴對方「That's easy for you to say.」

好說好用 1

W: I'm going to Harvard.
我要去讀哈佛大學。

M: That's easy for you to say.
你說得倒輕鬆。

W: You could go too if your grades were better.
如果你的成績好一點，你也可以去。

M: That's wishful thinking.
那是一個夢想。

好說好用 2

M: I think we should go camping this weekend.
我認為我們這個週末應該去露營。

W: That's easy for you to say.
你說得倒輕鬆。

M: Why?
為什麼？

W: Because you don't have to work for a living.
因為你不必為生活工作。

M: I work.
我也在工作。

W: Only when you want to.
只有當你想做時。

好說好用 **3**

W: I can't wait until prom.
我等不及畢業舞會到來。

M: That's easy for you to say, but I don't have a date.
你說得倒輕鬆，但是我沒有舞伴。

W: What about Mary?
瑪麗怎麼樣？

M: Do you think she would go with me?
你認為她會跟我去嗎？

單字慣用語

☑ grade	[gred]	成績
☑ go camping		去露營
☑ prom	[prɑm]	畢業舞會

What can I tell you?
你要我說什麼？

「What can I tell you?」這句話的意思是問對方「你要我說什麼？」

好說好用 1

M: I need to know if she likes me.
我需要知道她是否喜歡我。

W: What can I tell you?
你要我說什麼？

M: Just tell me if she ever talks about me.
只要告訴我她有沒有提到我。

W: She does sometimes.
她有時候會提到你。

M: Well, what does she say?
那，她說什麼？

W: She says she thinks you are cute.
她說她認為你很帥。

好說好用 2

W: What can I tell you?
你要我說什麼？

M: Tell me what you learned in school today.
告訴我今天你在學校學到什麼。

W: We learned about geography.
我們學地理。

M: Then where is Bora Bora.
那麼告訴我，波拉波拉在哪裡。

好說好用 3

M: I need some information.
我需要一些消息。

W: What can I tell you?
你要我說什麼？

M: Where is the nearest bank?
最近的銀行在哪裡？

W: Down the street to the right.
從這條街走下去，在右邊。

單字慣用語

☑ information	[ˌɪnfɚˈmeʃən]	消息
☑ right	[raɪt]	右邊
☑ cute	[kjut]	帥
☑ geography	[dʒiˈɑɡrəfɪ]	地理

What can I tell you?
你要我怎麼說呢？

易開竅

在本單元中，「What can I tell you?」是用在問對方「你要我怎麼說呢？」和上一個單元的意思不同。

好說好用 1

W: How could something like this have happened?
像這樣的事是怎麼發生的？

M: I don't know.
我不知道。

W: You lied to me.
你說謊。

M: What can I tell you?
你要我怎麼說呢？

I'm sorry.
我很抱歉。

W: Sorry is not good enough.
抱歉還不夠。

M: Well, then what can I tell you?
那，你要我怎麼說呢？

好說好用 2

M: I cut my leg riding that motorcycle.
我騎摩托車時割傷了我的腿。

W: What can I tell you?
你要我怎麼說呢？

You shouldn't have been riding it in the first place.
你原本就不應該騎的。

M: But, it was fun.
但是，那很好玩。

W: Yes, until you cut your leg.
是啊，割傷了腿就不好玩了。

好說好用 3

W: What can I tell you?
你要我怎麼說呢？

My new boyfriend is just wonderful.
我的新男朋友好棒。

M: I'm so happy for you.
我很替你高興。

W: Me, too.
我也是。

M: What is he like?
他長得怎麼樣？

單字慣用語

☑ lied   [laɪd]   說謊（lie 的過去式）

☑ motorcycle   [ˈmotɚˌsaɪkl̩]   摩托車

MEMO

What do you say?
你怎麼說？

 MP3 -62

易開竅

「What do you say?」是一句問對方意見的話。

好說好用 1

M: What do you say about the new bill?
有關新的法案，你的看法如何？

W: I'm not really familiar with that issue.
那個問題我不太清楚。

M: It's on the news every night.
每天晚上新聞都有。

W: I don't watch the news.
我不看新聞。

M: You need to get better informed.
你需要多吸收一點消息。

W: Does that stuff really affect me?
那件事對我真的有影響嗎？

好說好用 2

W: What do you say to a nice cup of coffee?
來一杯咖啡如何？

M: That sounds wonderful.
聽起來不錯。

W: It does to me, too.
對我來說也是。

I'll go make some.
我去泡一些。

M: Great.
好棒。

好說好用 3

M: So, what do you say?
那，你怎麼說？

W: About what?
關於什麼事？

M: About going out with me this weekend.
這個週末跟我出去。

W: All right.
好吧。

單字慣用語

☑ familiar	[fə'mɪljɚ]	熟悉
☑ issue	['ɪʃʊ]	問題
☑ informed	[ɪn'fɔrmd]	提供消息（inform 的過去分詞）
☑ stuff	[stʌf]	事情

What a shame.
那真可惜。

「What a shame.」是用在聽到或看到不好的消息時，安慰對方的話。

好說好用 1

M: I was planning on going to the ball game.
我本來計畫好要去參加球賽。

But I can't get off of work.
但是我被工作絆住了。

W: What a shame.
那真可惜。

M: Yes, I really wanted to go.
是啊，我真的很想去。

W: I wanted you to go, too.
我也希望你去。

好說好用 2

W: Mary wrecked her brand new car.
瑪麗撞壞了她那部嶄新的車子。

M: Oh, what a shame.
噢，好可惜。

W: Yes, but at least she wasn't hurt.
是啊，但至少她沒有受傷。

M: I'm glad to hear that.
我很高興聽到那樣。

好說好用 3

M: What a shame, you ruined your brand new dress.
好可惜，你把你的新衣服弄髒了。

W: I know.
我知道。

M: Do you think the stain will come out?
你認為這污點洗得掉嗎？

W: I doubt it.
這我很懷疑。

單字慣用語

☑ wrecked	[rɛkt]	撞壞（wreck 的過去式）
☑ ruined	[ruɪnd]	弄髒（ruin 的過去式）
☑ brand new		嶄新的
☑ stain	[sten]	污點

What about it?

有什麼問題嗎？

🔘 *MP3-64*

易開竅

「What about it?」是用來問對方關於某件事或某個人有什麼問題，或有什麼不同的意見。

好說好用 1

M: Let's go to the beach.
讓我們到海邊去。

W: Oh, I don't know.
噢，我不知道。

M: Come on, what about it?
來吧，你有什麼問題嗎？

W: Well, okay.
嗯，好吧。

好說好用 2

W: Do you know that blue sweater of yours?
你知道你的那件藍色毛衣嗎？

M: Yes, what about it?
知道，有什麼問題嗎？

W: Can I borrow it?
我可以借嗎？

M: No.
不行。

W: Why not?
為什麼不行？

M: Because you'll lose it.
因為你會把它弄丟。

好說好用 3

M: Do you know that girl over there?
你知道那邊那個女孩嗎？

W: Yes, what about her?
知道，她怎麼啦？

M: She is a snob.
她很勢利。

W: Yes, she is.
她是很勢利。

單字慣用語

☐ snob	[snɑb]	勢利的人
☐ sweater	[ˈswɛtɚ]	毛衣
☐ beach	[bitʃ]	海邊

Who knows?
誰知道？

MP3-65

易開竅

　　當有人提出問題，你不知道問題的答案，但你有一種也想知道該問題的答案，卻似乎有沒人知道的無可奈何感時，就可以回答「Who knows?」。

好說好用 1

W: When will she have our papers graded?
她何時會把我們的報告打好分數？

M: Who knows?
誰知道？

W: I want to know what I made.
我想知道我得幾分。

M: Me too.
我也是。

好說好用 2

M: Do you know what we're having for dinner?
你知道我們晚餐要吃什麼嗎？

W: Who knows — it could be anything.
誰知道—什麼都有可能。

M: Maybe we'll dine out.
或許我們會去外面吃。

W: That's a good idea.
那是個好主意。

好說好用 3

W: What is he up to now?
他想做什麼？

M: Who knows?
誰知道？

W: He is always getting in trouble.
他總是惹麻煩。

M: I know.
我知道。

W: Can't you control him?
你沒辦法控制他嗎？

M: He's your son too.
他也是你的兒子。

Who's there?
是誰在那兒？

🔘 *MP3-66*

易 開 竅

這句話是用在門外有人敲門或按門鈴時，你在門內先問，「是誰在那兒？」（或「門外是誰？」）

好說好用 1

M: Did you hear the door?
你聽到敲門聲嗎？

W: Yes, who is it?
聽到了，是誰？

M: I don't know.
我不知道。

W: Well, find out.
那就去看看。

M: Who's there?
是誰在那兒？

W: It's Mary.
我是瑪麗。

好說好用 2

W: Knock knock.
敲門。

M: Who's there?
是誰啊？

W: It's Mary.
我是瑪麗。

M: Oh, hi Mary.
噢，嗨，瑪麗。

好說好用 3

M: Who's there?
是誰在那兒？

W: I think it is John.
我想是約翰。

M: I don't want to see him.
我不想見他。

W: So, don't answer the door.
那就別應門。

好說好用 4

M: Who was it at the door?
剛剛是誰在門外？

W: It was Mary.
是瑪麗。

M: What did she want?
她要做什麼？

W: She wanted to borrow an egg.
她要借個雞蛋。

單字慣用語

☑ knock	[nɑk]	敲門
☑ borrow	['bɑro]	借
☑ answer the door		應門

MEMO

What I'm saying is...

我在說……

易開竅
🔘 *MP3 -67*

強調或是重複你現在在說的話，用「What I am saying is
＋你在說的話」。

好說好用 1

W: So, what are you saying?
那，你在說什麼？

M: What I'm saying is that I like you.
我在說「我喜歡妳」。

W: I like you, too.
我也喜歡你。

M: I'm glad.
我很高興。

好說好用 2

M: What I'm saying is that you are going to get in
trouble.
我說的是，你會惹麻煩的。

W: Not if you don't tell on me.
如果你不去告發我的話就不會。

M: But what you are doing is wrong.
但是你現在在做的是不對的。

W: I don't think so.
我不這麼想。

M: All I'm saying is be careful.
我要說的就是「小心點」。

W: I will.
我會的。

好說好用 3

W: What are you trying to say?
你到底想說什麼？

M: I'm saying I would like to go on a date with you.
我說我想約你出去。

W: Really?
真的嗎？

M: Yes.
是真的。

單字慣用語

☑ trouble   [ˈtrʌbl̩]   麻煩

☑ tell on someone   洩漏他人秘密

You bet.
好的。（是的。）

易開竅

「You bet.」是一句用法很廣泛的口語，原本的意思是「你可以很確定」。當有人向你提出要求時，你可以說「You bet.」，表示你答應。或是有人向你說「Thank you.」時，你也可以回答「You bet.」。

好說好用 1

M: Can you give me a ride home?
你可以載我回家嗎？

W: You bet.
好的。

M: Do you know how to get to my house?
你知道如何到我家嗎？

W: Yes.
知道。

好說好用 2

W: Do you think she will win 1st prize?
你認為她會贏得首獎嗎？

M: Sure, didn't you vote for her?
當然，你沒有投給她嗎？

W: You bet.
有的。

M: Good, me too.
很好，我也是。

好說好用 3

M: Lunch is on me today.
今天的午飯我請客。

W: Really?
真的嗎？

M: You bet.
真的。

W: Then let's go to Seafood King.
那我們到海鮮大王去。

M: Wait, I don't have that much money.
等等，我沒有那麼多錢。

W: All right.
好吧。

單字慣用語

☑ prize	[praɪz]	獎品
☑ vote for		投票給

You can count on me.
你可以信任我。

 MP3 -69

易 開 竅

　「You can count on me.」是一句用在答應對方要做某件事之後，又再向對方提出保證，以使對方安心的話。

好說好用 1

W: Will you be here at 8:00 to help me?
你可以八點鐘到這兒來幫我嗎？

M: Sure.
可以。

W: Do you promise?
你一定會來嗎？

M: You can count one me.
你可以信任我。

W: Thank you. I really appreciate it.
謝謝你，我真的很感激。

M: You bet.
不客氣。

好說好用 2

W: You can count on me to be here at 8:00.
你可以信得過我，我八點一定會到這裡。

M: I know I can.
我知道我可以信得過你。

W: If there is anything I can do, let me know.
如果有什麼我可以幫你做的，讓我知道。

M: I will. Thank you.
我會的。謝謝你。

MEMO

You just watch!
你等著瞧！

🔘 *MP3-70*

易開竅

「You just watch!」是用在對方不相信你說你能做的，於是你要對方等著瞧，你會做給他看。

好說好用 1

M: I'll bet you can't hop all the way to that line.
我打賭你不能一路用單腳跳到那條線。

W: You just watch.
你等著瞧好了。

M: Go ahead.
那你就做吧。

W: Here I go.
我來了。

M: Wow, you did it.
哇，你做到了。

W: I told you.
我跟你說過的。

好說好用 2

W: Watch.
你看著。

M: Where did you learn to do that?
你在哪裡學會那麼做的？

W: I learned it in dance class.
我在舞蹈課學的。

M: Teach me.
你教我。

好說好用 3

M: I'll bet you can't do this.
我打賭你不會做。

W: Oh yeah, watch me.
哦，是嗎？看著我。

M: I told you couldn't do it.
我說過你不會做的。

W: Let me try again.
讓我再試一次。

M: No.
不。

W: Yes, watch.
可以的，你看著。

單字慣用語

☑ hop	[hɑp]	v. 用單腳跳
☑ line	[laɪn]	n. 線

Unit 70

You know what?
你知道嗎？

易開竅

MP3-71

「You know what?」是一句用來打開話題的話。

好說好用 1

M: You know what?
你知道嗎？

W: What?
什麼事？

M: The teacher says I'm her favorite.
老師說我是她最喜歡的。

W: Oh, yeah, well she told me the same thing.
是嘛，她也這麼對我說。

M: She did not.
她沒有。

W: How do you know?
你怎麼知道？

好說好用 2

W: Hey, do you know what?
嘿，你知道嗎？

M: What?
什麼事？

W: I'm going to Japan over Spring Break.
春假我要去日本。

M: That's great!
那很棒！

好說好用 3

M: You know what?
你知道嗎？

W: No.
不知道。

M: I don't like that new girl in school.
我不喜歡學校裡那個新來的女孩。

W: You know what?
你知道嗎？

M: What?
什麼？

W: Me either.
我也不喜歡。

單字慣用語

☑ favorite	['fævərɪt]	最喜歡的
☑ either	['iðɚ]	也不

It seems...
似乎……

MP3-72

易開窺

「It seems」表示「某件事看起來好像是如此」。在說一件事之前加上「It seems」，是英語會話的說法之一，沒有把話講得很死，如此的說法含有邀請對方表達意見的意味，對方一聽你這麼說，多半會有回應，如此話題就打開了。

好說好用 1

M: It seems these copiers have gone up in price.
似乎這些影印機的價格都漲價了。

W: They have.
是漲價了。

You should have bought one before the price increased last month.
你在上個月漲價之前就應該買一個。

M: We couldn't afford it then.
那時候我們沒有錢。

W: Well, they really aren't that much more expensive.
是嗎，它們其實也沒有貴多少。

And they are still the same excellent quality.
在品質上它們還是一樣的。

好說好用 2

W: It seems we'll be working together next week.
看起來下個禮拜我們似乎要一起工作了。

M: How nice!
那真好！

Did the principal team us up?
是校長把我們弄成一組的嗎？

W: Yes, he thought our teaching styles complimented each other.
是的。他認為我們的教學型態可以互補。

M: I agree.
我同意。

It will be a pleasure teaching beside you!
在你身旁與你一起教書真是榮幸！

好說好用 3

M: It seems you have a mild case of the flu.
似乎你得了輕微的流行性感冒。

W: I do feel awful.
我真的覺得很不舒服。

M: You'll have to get plenty of rest and drink lots of fluids.
你必須要充分地休息，並且喝很多的水。

W: How long will it last?
這個感冒會維持多久呢？

M: About two weeks, if you take care of yourself.
大概兩星期，如果好好照顧自己的話。

W: Thank you, Doctor.
謝謝你，醫生。

單字慣用語

☑ copier	['kɑpɪɚ]	影印機
☑ afford	[ə'fɔrd]	付得起錢
☑ flu	[flu]	流行性感冒
☑ plenty	['plɛntɪ]	很多
☑ fluids	[fluɪdz]	水分
☑ to go up in price		價格上漲
☑ teamed up with		與（某人）一組

MEMO

I wonder if...
我在猜想……

MP3-73

易開竅

　　想要問對方問題，不一定非用傳統的疑問句不可，本單元教你另一種問法：「I wonder if」這個句型，表面上的意思是「我在猜想」或「我懷疑」，其實就是在問對方了。這種問法大都用在你也沒把握對方會給你肯定的答案。例如：你們去找人，敲了門卻沒人應門，你不知道有沒有人在家（if anyone is home），而你知道跟你去的朋友也不會知道，所以你就說「I wonder if anyone is home.」（我懷疑是不是有人在家。）

好說好用 1

M: Did you knock at the door?
　　你有沒有敲門呢？

W: Yes, but no one is answering.
　　有的，但是沒有人回答。

M: I wonder if anyone is home?
　　我在懷疑是不是有人在家？

W: I think so.
　　我想有人。

　　There's a car in the driveway and the lights are on.
　　車道上有車，並且燈還是亮著的。

好說好用 2

W: I wonder if he's married.
我懷疑他是不是已經結婚了。

M: Don't get your hopes up.
不要抱太大的希望。

He's probably got a wonderful wife at home.
他家裡也許有一個很好的太太呢。

W: Still, there's no harm in asking.
縱然是這樣，問一問也不會有傷害呀。

M: Why don't you set your sights on someone else?
你為什麼不把眼光朝別人看呢？

W: Maybe I should.
也許我應該這樣子做。

He looks out of my league, anyway.
反正看起來我也高攀不上他。

好說好用 3

W: I wonder if we will get the day off on Friday?
我在想我們是不是星期五也請假？

M: You mean because it's a three-day weekend?
你的意思是說因為我們有三天的週末。

W: Yes.
是的。

It would be nice to have an extra day.
能多出一天那會很好。

M: We do deserve it, but don't count on it.
我們是應該多放一天假，不過，不要抱太大希望。

The boss has had a bad week and is in no mood to give us anything extra.
老闆這個星期並不順利，並且也沒那個心情給我們額外的東西。

單字慣用語

☑ knock	[nɑk]	敲門
☑ driveway	[ˈdraɪˌwe]	車道
☑ league	[lig]	同輩；聯盟
☑ harm	[hɑrm]	傷害
☑ three-day weekend		三天長週末
☑ set your sights		把目光注視於
☑ out of one's league		超過（某人）的層次

I believe...
我相信……

易開竅

🔵 *MP3 -74*

在你要說的一件事之前加上「I believe」，跟說一件事之前加句「It seems」的用法一樣，是英語會話中常用的，比只說該事件多點其他的意味。用「I believe」帶有「要對方安心」的味道，例如：對方兩點鐘要開會，但他在一點半時卻嚷著遲到了，你不僅要告訴他才一點半，還要叫他安心，確實是一點半而已，這時你不要只是說「It's only 1:30 now.」，而是要說「I believe it's only 1:30 now.」。

用「I believe」還有要告訴對方「情況確實是如此」的意思，例如：你把對方要的文件給他了，但是他又來跟你要，此時你應該說「I believe I gave it to you.」（我相信我已經給你了。）這句話的語氣比只說「I gave it to you.」更有不容置疑的意味。

好說好用 1

M: I am running late!
我的時間遲了。

W: What time do you have to be at the conference?
你幾時要參加會議呢？

M: Two o'clock.
兩點。

W: I believe it's only 1:30 now.
我相信現在才一點半啊。

M: Good.
那很好。

The conference is not very far.
會議的地點不很遠。

W: Then don't worry, you won't be late.
那就不要擔心,你不會遲到的。

好說好用 2

W: Excuse me, but I believe you are sitting in my seat.
對不起,但我相信你坐的是我的座位。

M: Let me check my ticket.
讓我看看我的票。

W: My ticket says I have seat 44B.
我的票顯示我的座位是 44B。

M: Oh, I am so sorry!
哦,真對不起!

I am supposed to be in seat 44A.
我應該是坐在 44A。

好說好用 3

W: Sir, I believe you left your umbrella on the bus.
先生,我相信你把雨傘遺留在公車上了。

M: You are right!
你説得對！

I will need it in the rain.
下雨我是需要雨傘的。

W: I brought it with me.
那我幫你帶過來了。

Here you go.
給你吧。

M: Thank you.
謝謝你。

That was very kind of you.
你真好心。

W: You're welcome.
不用客氣。

單字慣用語

☑ watch	[wɑtʃ]	手錶
☑ check	[tʃɛk]	檢查
☑ umbrella	[ʌm'brɛlə]	雨傘
☑ kind	[kaɪnd]	仁慈
☑ left	[lɛft]	遺留
☑ to run late		遲到
☑ supposed to		應該

Has the bus for downtown left yet?
到市區的公車開走了沒有？

MP3-75

　　我們常常會遇到需要問「某件事情發生了沒？」或「某件事情好了沒？」遇到這種情況，記住這個句型「Has/Have + 某事 + 動詞的過去分詞 + yet?」例如問：「公車開走了沒有？」公車開走 (leave) 的過去分詞是「left」，所以句子就是「Has the bus left yet?」。例句中説的是「到市區」的公車（the bus for downtown），所以完整的句子是「Has the bus for downtown left yet?」。

　　在「好説好用 1」中，問的是「我所訂的書進來了嗎？」書進來 (come in) 的過去分詞也是「come in」，所以句子是「Has the book come in yet?」；至於「我所訂的書」，是「the book I ordered」，所以完整的句子就是「Has the book I ordered come in yet?」。

　　在「好説好用 2」中，問的是對方，而不是某件事，我們把學過的句型稍微改一下，變成「Has/Have + 某人 + 動詞的過去分詞 + yet?」。如果你要問的是「你想出答案沒有？」想出（figure out）的過去分詞是「figured out」，所以句子是「Have you figured out the answer yet?」。

好說好用 1

M: Has the book I ordered come in yet?
我所訂的書進來了嗎？

W: Let me call up your account on the computer.
讓我在電腦上把你的帳戶叫出來。

M: I have been waiting for two weeks.
我已經等了兩個星期了。

W: Yes, I have found it.
我已經找到了。

You can pick it up at the register.
你可以到櫃檯去拿。

好說好用 2

W: Have you figured out the answer to problem six yet?
你已經想出第六題的答案沒有？

M: No, that's a tough one.
還沒有，那是很困難的一題。

W: I spent all night working on it.
我整個晚上就在做那一題。

M: Let's ask the professor to help us.
我們要求教授幫我們解答吧。

好說好用 3

M: Has the package arrived yet?
包裹到了沒有？

W: No.
還沒有。

I called the post office.
我打電話到郵局了。

M: What did they say?
他們怎麼說？

W: They said it should arrive this Saturday.
他們說應該禮拜六會到。

M: Good!
很好！

That will be just in time for the birthday party.
那還可以趕上生日宴會。

單字慣用語

☑ order	[ˈɔrdɚ]	訂購
☑ problem	[ˈprɑbləm]	問題
☑ professor	[prəˈfɛsɚ]	教授
☑ package	[ˈpækɪdʒ]	包裹
☑ post office		郵局
☑ figure out		想出結果
☑ just in time		即時

I thought...
我以為……

易開竅

🔘 *MP3-76*

　　有時你會遇到發生的情況跟你所預期的不同，此時，英語的基本句型就是「I thought + 你原本認為的情況」。注意！當你說這句話時，「我想」或「我以為」已經是過去了，所以要說「I thought」。「thought」是「think」（以為）的過去式。例如：本單元的例句「I thought I was late.」（我以為我遲到了。）說明了事實上你並沒有遲到，但你原本以為你遲到了。

　　又如在「好說好用 1」中，W 問 M「你把眼鏡放在哪裡？」W 認為他是把眼鏡放在桌上，可是桌上並沒有，所以回答「I thought I put them on my desk.」（我想我把它放在桌上啊。）或是在「好說好用 3」中，M 原本交代 W「make two copies of this letter」（把信複印兩份）但 W 只複印了一份，所以 M 說「I thought I told you to make two copies of this letter.」（我想我告訴過你這封信要複印兩份的。）

　　「I thought + 一件事情」，也可以表示你計畫這麼做，例如在「好說好用 2」中，因為 W 很累了，所以她計畫要早點去睡覺，說法是「I thought I would go to bed early tonight.」（我想我今晚要早點去睡覺。）

好說好用 1

M: Have you seen my glasses?
你有沒有看到我的眼鏡？

W: No.
沒有。

Where did you put them?
你把它放在哪裡？

M: I thought I put them on my desk.
我想我把它放在桌子上啊。

W: Here they are.
哦，就在這裡。

Someone covered them with a newspaper.
我想有人用報紙把它們蓋起來了。

好說好用 2

W: Goodnight.
晚安。

I thought I would go to bed early tonight.
我想我今晚要早點去睡覺。

M: Are you really tired?
你真的累了嗎？

W: Yes.
是的。

I have been working extra hours at the office.
我今天在辦公室加了班。

M: Well, some extra sleep will do you good.
好吧，多睡一下對你比較好。

好說好用 3

M: I thought I told you to make two copies of this letter.
我想我告訴過你這封信要複印兩份的。

W: You need two copies?
你需要兩份嗎？

M: Yes, one for Mr. Brown.
是的，一份給布朗先生。

And one for Mrs. Smith.
另外一份給史蜜絲太太。

W: I will make them for you right away.
我馬上就幫你去做。

單字慣用語

☐ glasses	['glæsɪz]	眼鏡
☐ cover	['kʌvɚ]	遮掩
☐ newspaper	['njuz,pepɚ]	報紙
☐ extra	['ɛkstrə]	額外的
☐ copy	['kɑpɪ]	份數
		（複數形：copies）
☐ do you good		對你有好處
☐ right away		馬上

Do you mind if...

Unit
76
你介意……

MP3-77

易開竅

當你想做一件事情，但這件事情會影響到別人，所以你要先問一下對方是否同意，標準的句型就是「Do you mind if + 你想做的事情？」（我想這麼做，你介意嗎？）例如：你看到一個空位，雖然你大可以坐下去，但有些場合你要表現得文明一點，禮貌上問一下鄰座的 人：「我坐這個位子 (if I sit down)，你介意嗎？」

「Do you mind if I sit down？」或是你想開窗戶 (open a window)，但不知道別人是否介意，同樣是這個句型：「Do you mind if I open a window？」。

好說好用 1

M: Do you mind if I sit down?
我坐下你介意嗎？

W: No, go right ahead.
不，儘管坐吧。

M: Thank you.
謝謝你。

It took a long time to find a seat.
我找好久才找到一個座位。

W: This meeting is very crowded.
這個會議人很多。

好說好用 2

W: It is so stuffy in here!
這裡好悶噢！

M: I think the air conditioning is out.
我想冷氣壞了。

W: Do you mind if I open a window?
我把窗戶打開，你介意嗎？

M: That's fine.
沒有問題。

Open the shade, too.
把百葉窗也拉開吧。

好說好用 3

M: Do you mind if I use your phone?
你介意我使用你的電話嗎？

W: Is it a local call?
是市內電話嗎？

M: No, it's long distance, but I have my calling card.
不，是長途電話。不過我用電話卡的號碼。

W: That's fine.
那就沒問題。

Use the phone in the room.
用房間裡的電話吧。

It's more private.
那支電話比較有隱私。

單字慣用語

☑ crowded	[ˈkraʊdɪd]	擁擠
☑ stuffy	[ˈstʌfɪ]	悶得透不過氣
☑ air conditioning	[ˈɛr kənˈdɪʃənɪŋ]	冷氣；空調
☑ local	[ˈlokl̩]	本地的
☑ private	[ˈpraɪvɪt]	有隱私的
☑ took a long time		花很多時間
☑ long distance		長途

MEMO

Is the meeting running on schedule?

會議會準時開始嗎？

易開竅　　　　　　　　　　　　　　🔘 *MP3 -78*

「on schedule」是個片語，意思是「按照原定的時間」。很多時候我們會問，某件事情是否按照原定的時間進行，這句話的基本句型就是「Is + 某件事 + 動詞的現在分詞 + on schedule?」。

例如問：「會議會準時進行（run）嗎？」就是「Is the meeting running on schedule?」，句中的進行（run）改成現在分詞「running」。

又如問「408 班機（Flight 408）會按預定時間抵達（arrive）嗎？」說法就是「Is Flight 408 arriving on schedule?」。

除了用上述的句型外，也可以用「Is + 某件事 + going to + 原形動詞 + on schedule?」

例如：把「Is the meeting running on schedule?」改成「Is the meeting going to run on schedule?」也可以。「好說好用 2」中的「Is the building going to be finished on schedule?」就是採用這個句型，問的是「這棟大樓會按照預定時間完成（be finished）嗎？」

好說好用 1

M: Is the meeting running on schedule?
會議會準時開始嗎？

W: Yes, it starts in five minutes.
是的，會議五分鐘內開始。

M: It's a good thing I got here on time!
還好我準時抵達這裡。

W: Yes, the company CEO will be speaking at the meeting today.
公司總經理會在今天的會議上講話。

好說好用 2

M: Is the building going to be finished on schedule?
這棟大樓會按照預定時間完成嗎？

W: I don't know.
我不清楚。

I'm going to call the builder tomorrow.
我明天要打電話給建築商。

M: I can't wait to be in my new office.
我等不及要搬到我的新辦公室。

W: The new building will be much roomier.
新的大樓會寬敞得多。

好說好用 3

W: Is Flight 408 arriving on schedule?
408 班機會按預定時間抵達嗎？

M: Yes, it is due to arrive at 6:58 p.m.
是的，它預計在下午六點五十八分抵達。

W: At which gate will it arrive, please?
請問它會抵達哪個機門？

M: Gate 43, Terminal 2.
二號航空站，第四十三號機門。

W: Is that by Baggage Claim?
那是在行李提領處的旁邊嗎？

M. Yes, it is across from Baggage Claim.
是的，它就在行李提領處對面。

單字慣用語

☑ CEO	[ˈsi i ˈo]	總經理
☑ terminal	[ˈtɝmənḷ]	航空站
☑ builder	[ˈbɪldɚ]	建築商
☑ baggage claim	[ˈbægɪdʒ ˈklem]	行李提領處
☑ roomier	[ˈrumɪɚ]	較寬敞
☑ It's a good thing...		還好；好在
☑ on time		準時

Unit 78

I hope...
我希望……

 MP3-79

易開竅

這個句型跟前面學過的「It seems...」或「I believe...」這兩個句型一樣,在所說的一件事情前面加一句「I hope」,表示這件事你也沒把握會成,但「I hope」表達了你對這件事的期待。例如:「我希望今天下午會下雨。」就是「I hope it rains this afternoon.」。

好說好用 1

M: Did you hear the weather this morning?
你今天早上聽氣象報告沒有?

W: They said we have a 30% chance of showers today.
報告中說今天有百分之三十的機會下雨。

M: Really?
真的嗎?

I don't see any clouds.
我沒看見有雲啊。

W: I hope it rains this afternoon.
我希望今天下午下雨。

M: Me, too.
我也是。

My lawn is dry.
我的草皮太乾了。

好說好用 2

W: I hope you are not going to wear that tie!
我希望你不會真的戴那條領帶。

M: Why not?
為什麼不戴。

I like it.
我喜歡它啊。

W: It doesn't look professional.
它看起來不夠專業感。

M: All right.
好吧。

How about this blue one?
這條藍色的如何？

W: That looks much better with your suit.
那一條看起來跟你的西裝配得較好。

好說好用 3

W: Are you ready for the exam today?
你準備好今天的考試了嗎？

M: Yes, I studied all week.
是的。我整星期都在讀書。

W: I hope it's not an essay test.
我希望考試不要有問答題。

M: Why not?
為什麼不要？

W: I do better on multiple-choice tests.
我選擇題考得比較好。

單字慣用語

☑ chance   [tʃæns]   機會

☑ showers   [ʃaʊɚz]   陣雨

☑ lawn   [lɔn]   草坪

☑ essay   [ˈɛse]   論說文

☑ multiple-choice   [ˌmʌltɪpl̩ˈtʃɔɪs] 選擇題

☑ how about...   （某物）可以嗎？

☑ to do better   表現較好

The park sure is quiet today.
今天公園好安靜喲！

易開窯

　　學英語不僅是要說得順口，還要讓外國人覺得你說得很道地，聽起來親切自然，那你與外國人不管是談生意或是交朋友，自然會無往不利。想要達到這個境界並不難，例如本單元要教你的，你與外國朋友到了公園，你覺得今天公園好寧靜，如果你說「The park is quiet today.」，整句話就顯得很單調，但如果你說「The park sure is quiet today.」，加個「sure」強調公園的安靜，氣氛就完全不同了。

　　在下面三個標準會話中，「The sky sure is getting dark.」的「sure」強調天色暗。「That sure is a nice new car!」的「sure」強調這部新車很好。「This dress sure is tight!」的「sure」強調洋裝太緊了。

　　在必要時加個「sure」，句子就生動多了！

好說好用 1

M: The sky sure is getting dark.
天空越來越黑了！

W: We are in for a big storm.
大暴風雨就要來了。

M: Did you close your car windows?
你車窗關了沒有？

W: Yes, they're all set.
有，它們都關好了。

好說好用 2

W: That sure is a nice new car!
好棒的新車喲！

M: It's a pleasure to drive.
開起來舒服得很。

W: Is it an automatic?
是自動排檔嗎？

M: Yes.
是的。

I never learned how to drive a stick.
我從沒學過開手排檔的車。

好說好用 3

W: This dress sure is tight!
這件套裝好緊哪！

M: Maybe you bought the wrong size.
也許你買錯尺寸了。

W: The tag says "size 10".
標籤上說是「十號」嘛。

M: Well, maybe it shrunk when you washed it.
是嗎？也許經你一洗它就縮水了。

單字慣用語

☑ automatic   [ˌɔtə'mætɪk]   （口語）自動排檔的車

☑ stick   [stɪk]   手排檔（操縱桿）

☑ tight   [taɪt]   緊

☑ size   [saɪz]   尺碼

☑ shrunk   [ʃrʌnk]   縮小

☑ all set   全弄好了

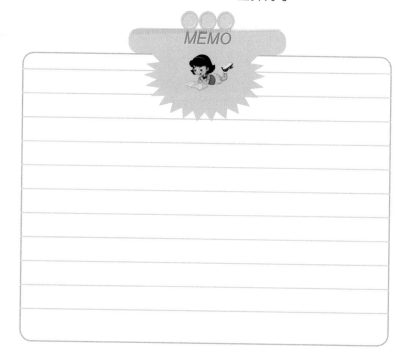

MEMO

I did not mean to...
我不是故意……

🔘 *MP3-81*

　　在日常生活中總是會有因為你不小心而妨害到別人的時候，這個時候道歉的方法之一就是表明「我不是故意這麼做的。」它的英語句型是「I didn't mean to + 你不小心所做的事.」例如：你不小心把咖啡灑在別人的身上（spill coffee on...）時，你就要趕緊說「I didn't mean to spill my coffee on you.」。

　　這個句型還可以用在別人在講話，但你必須插嘴時。這時雖然你不是不小心做了妨害到別人的事，但打斷別人的談話（interrupt）也同樣會妨害到別人，所以你也可以借用本單元的基本句型說：「I didn't mean to interrupt.」（我不是有意要打岔。）

好說好用 1

M: Oops!
哎呀！

I did not mean to spill my drink on you!
我不是故意要把飲料潑在你身上。

W: Do you have a napkin?
你有沒有餐巾？

M: Here's one.
這裡有一條。

Let me help you.
讓我幫你吧。

W: Thanks.
謝謝。

M: May I have your jacket cleaned for you?
可以讓我把你的外套送洗嗎？

W: No, thank you.
謝謝，不用了。

I can wash it at home.
我可以在家洗。

好說好用 2

W: I did not mean to interrupt.
我不是有意要打岔。

M: It's all right.
沒有關係。

We were just finishing.
我們正好說完。

W: Was that your boss?
那是你主管嗎？

M: No, that was my partner.
不，是我的合夥人。

好說好用 3

M: Excuse me, I think you gave me incorrect change.
對不起，我想你找我的零錢不對。

W: How much did I give you?
我給你多少？

M: You gave me 5 dollars, but you owe me another ten.
你給我五元，還差我十元。

W: Did you give me a 20?
你給我二十元嗎？

M: Yes.
是啊。

W: I'm sorry.
我很對不起。

I did not mean to short change you.
我不是故意少找你零錢。

單字慣用語

☑ spill	[spɪl]	打翻（飲料）
☑ napkin	[ˈnæpkɪn]	餐巾
☑ interrupt	[ˌɪntəˈrʌpt]	打斷；打岔
☑ partner	[ˈpɑrtnɚ]	合夥人
☑ short-change	[ˌʃɔrtˈtʃændʒ]	少找零錢
☑ just finishing		剛好（做）完
☑ correct change		正確零錢
☑ at home		在家

附錄：單字慣用語總整理

☑ jar   [dʒɑr]   罐子

☑ tight   [taɪt]   緊

☑ escort   [ɪ'skɔrt]   護送

☑ allow   [ə'laʊ]   允許

☑ You bet.   好的。

☑ No problem.   沒問題。

☑ It's a date.   就這麼説定。

☑ hand   [hænd]   v. 遞過來

☑ towel   [taʊl]   毛巾

☑ beach   [bitʃ]   海邊

☑ swimsuit   ['swɪmsut]   游泳衣

☑ boss   [bɔs]   老闆

☑ You're welcome.   不用客氣。

☑ steady   ['stɛdɪ]   固定

☑ joking   ['dʒokɪŋ]   開玩笑

☑ test   [tɛst]   測驗

☑ crush   [krʌʃ]   （口語）熱戀

☑ go steady   做固定的男女朋友

☑ has a crush on...   喜歡上某人

☑ owe   [o]   欠

☑ dime   [daɪm]   十分錢

☑ voting   ['votɪŋ]   投票

☑ worthy   ['wɝðɪ]   值得的

☑ candidate   ['kændɪˌdet]   候選人

☑ disagree	[ˌdɪsə'gri]		不同意
☑ turn	[tɝn]		n. 輪流
☑ vote for			投票給（某人）
☑ rude	[rud]		沒禮貌
☑ complain	[kəm'plen]		抱怨
☑ stock	['stɑk]		存貨
☑ hold	[hold]		v. 留著
☑ in stock			有存貨
☑ catch	['kætʃ]		趕上
☑ meet	['mit]		見面
☑ Sounds good.			聽起來是個好主意
☑ enjoy	[ɪn'dʒɔɪ]		v. 喜歡
☑ visit	['vɪzɪt]		拜訪
☑ shopping	['ʃɑpɪŋ]		購物
☑ join	[dʒɔɪn]		加入
☑ seat	['sit]		座位
☑ have a seat			請坐
☑ after work			下班後
☑ all right			好的
☑ appointment	[ə'pɔɪntmənt]		約會
☑ spilled	[spɪld]		使溢出
☑ forgot	[fɚ'gɑt]		忘記
☑ oven	['ʌvən]		火爐
☑ guess	[gɛs]		猜想
☑ clean up			清理乾淨
☑ turn off			關掉

☑ clean	[klin]	v. 清理乾淨	
☑ grounded	[ˈɡraʊndɪd]	被禁止做某事	
☑ clear	[klɪr]	清楚	
☑ understand	[ˌʌndɚˈstænd]	瞭解	
☑ president	[ˈprɛzɪdənt]	總統	
☑ laugh	[læf]	笑	
☑ passed	[pæst]	v.（考試）及格	
☑ cute	[kjut]	漂亮	
☑ there is no way		不可能的	
☑ won	[wʌn]	贏（win 的過去式）	
☑ election	[ɪˈlɛkʃən]	選舉	
☑ probably	[ˈprɑbəblɪ]	可能	
☑ win	[wɪn]	贏	
☑ game	[ɡem]	比賽	
☑ wrapped up something		有充分的準備	
☑ lost	[lɔst]	v. 輸了	
☑ turn out		結果	
☑ spin	[spɪn]	急馳	
☑ wreck	[rɛk]	撞壞（車子）	
☑ ask someone out		約某人出去	
☑ go out with...		跟某人出去	
☑ come on		別這樣	
☑ not a chance		門都沒有	
☑ think about		考慮	
☑ guilty	[ˈɡɪltɪ]	有罪	
☑ contest	[ˈkɑntɛst]	比賽	

☑	better	[ˈbɛtɚ]	更好
☑	I guess so.		我想是吧
☑	horrible	[ˈhɔrəbl̩]	很糟
☑	bad	[bæd]	不好
☑	happened	[ˈhæpənd]	發生
☑	pizza	[ˈpitsə]	比薩餅
☑	extra	[ˈɛkstrə]	多餘的
☑	cheese	[tʃiz]	乳酪
☑	bother	[ˈbɑðɚ]	打擾
☑	smoke	[smok]	抽煙
☑	spend the night		過夜
☑	come over		過來
☑	straight	[stret]	連續的
☑	semester	[səˈmɛstɚ]	學期
☑	cheerleader	[ˈtʃɪrlidɚ]	啦啦隊
☑	absolutely	[ˈæbsəˌlutlɪ]	肯定地
☑	chicken v	[ˈtʃɪkən]	畏怯
☑	chicken out		臨陣退縮
☑	of course		當然
☑	skiing	[ˈskiɪŋ]	滑雪
☑	show	[ʃo]	表演
☑	midnight	[ˈmɪdˌnaɪt]	午夜
☑	go skiing		去滑雪
☑	hard	[hard]	嚴厲的
☑	mind	[maɪnd]	v. 介意
☑	drink	[drɪŋk]	飲料

☑ gross	[gros]	（食物）令人噁心的
☑ outfit	[ˈautˌfɪt]	服裝
☑ as long as		只要
☑ of course		當然
☑ soft drink		冷飲
☑ burglary	[ˈbɝglərɪ]	偷竊
☑ exciting	[ɪkˈsaɪtɪŋ]	令人興奮的
☑ mad	[mæd]	生氣
☑ doubt	[daʊt]	懷疑
☑ pants	[pænts]	褲子
☑ hole	[hol]	洞
☑ sew	[so]	縫補
☑ be mad at...		生氣
☑ had better		最好
☑ disrespectful	[ˌdɪsrɪˈspɛktfəl]	沒禮貌
☑ promise	[ˈpramɪs]	保證
☑ lie	[laɪ]	說謊
☑ locked	[ˈlakt]	鎖（lock 的過去分詞）
☑ learn the lesson		學到教訓
☑ come out of		出來
☑ locked up		鎖起來
☑ graduated	[ˈgrædʒuˌetɪd]	畢業
☑ congratulations	[kənˌgrætʃəˈleʃənz]	恭喜
☑ kindergarten	[ˈkɪndɚgartn̩]	幼稚園
☑ wear	[wɛr]	穿

☑	exam	[ɪɡˈzæm]	考試
☑	manage	[ˈmænɪdʒ]	設法做到
☑	next time		下一次
☑	bought	[bɔt]	買（buy 的過去式）
☑	found	[faʊnd]	找到（find 的過去式）
☑	department	[dɪˈpɑrtmənt]	部門
☑	jealous	[ˈdʒɛləs]	嫉妒
☑	boss	[bɔs]	老闆
☑	fire	[ˈfaɪr]	v. 解雇
☑	department store		百貨公司
☑	sports car		跑車
☑	quitting	[ˈkwɪtɪŋ]	停止（quit 的現在分詞）
☑	tripped	[trɪpt]	絆倒（trip 的過去分詞）
☑	weird	[wɪrd]	奇怪的
☑	parking lot		停車場
☑	summer camp		夏令營
☑	keep in touch		保持聯繫
☑	particular	[pɚˈtɪkjələ]	特別的
☑	assistance	[əˈsɪstəns]	幫忙
☑	show	[ʃo]	v. 拿來給（某人）看
☑	look for		尋找
☑	phone	[fon]	電話
☑	second	[ˈsɛkənd]	（口語）片刻
☑	gift	[ɡɪft]	禮物
☑	just one second		等一下

☑ inherit	[ɪnˈhɛrɪt]	繼承
☑ treat	[trit]	v. 請客
☑ in that case		如果是那樣的話
☑ go to a movie		去看電影
☑ appreciate	[əˈpriʃɪˌet]	感激
☑ give me a hand		幫我一個忙
☑ pick up someone		接某人
☑ address	[əˈdrɛs]	地址
☑ promise	[ˈpramɪs]	保證
☑ keep in touch with		跟某人保持聯絡
☑ lost touch		失去聯絡
☑ argument	[ˈargjəmənt]	爭執
☑ apologize	[əˈpalədʒaɪz]	道歉
☑ talk it over		討論它
☑ blow over		消失；過去
☑ insist	[ɪnˈsɪst]	堅持
☑ jacket	[ˈdʒækɪt]	夾克
☑ collar	[ˈkalɚ]	領子
☑ bartender	[ˈbarˌtɛndɚ]	酒保
☑ margarita	[ˌmargəˈritə]	瑪格麗特雞尾酒
☑ steak	[stek]	牛排
☑ medium	[ˈmidɪəm]	七分熟
☑ decide	[dɪˈsaɪd]	決定
☑ feature	[ˈfitʃɚ]	特點
☑ difficult	[ˈdɪfəkəlt]	困難的

☑	decision	[dɪˈsɪʒən]	決定
☑	wear	[wɛr]	穿
☑	responsible	[rɪˈspɑnsəbḷ]	負責的
☑	serious	[ˈsɪrɪəs]	認真的，不是開玩笑的
☑	miss	[mɪs]	錯過
☑	point	[pɔɪnt]	重點
☑	action film		動作片
☑	plan	[plæn]	計畫
☑	towel	[taʊl]	毛巾
☑	important	[ɪmˈpɔrtənt]	重要的
☑	mind	[maɪnd]	介意
☑	sweat	[swɛt]	流汗
☑	trash	[træʃ]	垃圾
☑	do the dishes		洗碗
☑	cover for		替人代班
☑	shift	[ʃɪft]	（班次）工作時間
☑	repay	[rɪˈpe]	報答
☑	raking	[ˈrekɪŋ]	耙（草）
☑	bag	[bæg]	v. 用袋子裝
☑	stuff	[stʌf]	事情
☑	go shopping		上街購物
☑	ride	[raɪd]	騎（腳踏車）
☑	bicycle	[ˈbaɪˌsɪkḷ]	腳踏車
☑	faster	[ˈfæstɚ]	更快
☑	cheat	[tʃit]	（考試）作弊

☑ apology	[ə'pɑlədʒɪ]	道歉
☑ climbed	[klaɪmd]	爬（climb 的過去式）
☑ mountain	['maʊntṇ]	山
☑ stay up		熬夜
☑ clean up		清理乾淨
☑ straight	[stret]	連續的
☑ flunked	[flʌŋkt]	（成績）不及格
☑ deserve	[dɪ'zɝv]	應受（懲罰或獎賞）
☑ well-behaved		很守規矩
☑ shame	[ʃem]	羞恥；丟臉
☑ mean	[min]	a. 刻薄的
☑ mean	[min]	v. 意欲
☑ upset	[ʌp'sɛt]	使不高興
☑ at least		至少
☑ get grounded		被罰不准做
☑ pool	[pul]	游泳池
☑ vacation	[ve'keʃən]	度假
☑ accident	['æksɪdənt]	車禍
☑ affect	[ə'fɛkt]	影響到
☑ rude	[rud]	沒禮貌
☑ none of your business		沒有你的事
☑ inviting	[ɪn'vaɪtɪŋ]	邀請
☑ glad	[glæd]	高興
☑ relax	[rɪ'læks]	放鬆
☑ while	[hwaɪl]	一段時間

☑	advice	[əd'vaɪs]	建議
☑	cold	[kold]	n. 感冒
☑	ankle	['æŋkḷ]	腳踝
☑	try out		選拔賽
☑	cheerleader	['tʃɪrlidɚ]	啦啦隊隊長
☑	horrible	['hɔrəbḷ]	（口語）糟透的
☑	shot	[ʃɑt]	注射
☑	mean	[min]	a. 刻薄的
☑	fell	[fɛl]	v. 跌倒
☑	guilty	['gɪltɪ]	內疚的
☑	offer	['ɔfɚ]	提供
☑	boss	[bɔs]	老闆
☑	promotion	[prə'moʃən]	晉級
☑	excited	[ɪk'saɪtɪd]	興奮的
☑	raise	[rez]	加薪
☑	prove	[pruv]	證明
☑	plate	[plet]	盤子
☑	graduating	['grædʒʊ,etɪŋ]	畢業
☑	final	['faɪnḷ]	最後的
☑	stand	['stænd]	忍受
☑	stereo	['stɛrɪo]	立體音響
☑	turn it down		轉小聲一點
☑	give up		放棄
☑	last	[læst]	最後的
☑	screw	[skru]	螺絲釘

☑ try out		試試看
☑ grade	[gred]	成績
☑ go camping		去露營
☑ prom	[prɑm]	畢業舞會
☑ information	[ˌɪnfɚˈmeʃən]	消息
☑ right	[raɪt]	右邊
☑ cute	[kjut]	帥
☑ geography	[dʒiˈɑgrəfɪ]	地理
☑ lied	[laɪd]	說謊
☑ motorcycle	[ˈmotɚˌsaɪkl̩]	摩托車
☑ familiar	[fəˈmɪljɚ]	熟悉
☑ issue	[ˈɪʃʊ]	問題
☑ informed	[ɪnˈfɔrmd]	提供消息
☑ stuff	[stʌf]	事情
☑ wrecked	[rɛkt]	撞壞
☑ ruined	[ruɪnd]	弄髒
☑ brand new		嶄新的
☑ stain	[sten]	污點
☑ snob	[snɑb]	勢利的人
☑ sweater	[ˈswɛtɚ]	毛衣
☑ beach	[bitʃ]	海邊
☑ knock	[nɑk]	敲門
☑ borrow	[ˈbɑro]	借
☑ answer the door		應門
☑ trouble	[ˈtrʌbl̩]	麻煩

☑ tell on someone		洩漏他人秘密
☑ prize	[praɪz]	獎品
☑ vote for		投票給
☑ hop	[hɑp]	v. 用單腳跳
☑ line	[laɪn]	n. 線
☑ favorite	[ˈfævərɪt]	最喜歡的
☑ either	[ˈiðɚ]	也不
☑ copier	[ˈkɑpɪɚ]	影印機
☑ afford	[əˈfɔrd]	付得起錢
☑ flu	[flu]	流行性感冒
☑ plenty	[ˈplɛntɪ]	很多
☑ fluids	[fluɪdz]	水分
☑ to go up in price		價格上漲
☑ teamed up with		與（某人）一組
☑ knock	[knɑk]	敲門
☑ driveway	[ˈdraɪvˌwe]	車道
☑ league	[lig]	同輩；聯盟
☑ harm	[hɑrm]	傷害
☑ three-day weekend		三天長週末
☑ set your sights		把目光注視於
☑ out of one's league		超過（某人）的層次
☑ watch	[wɑtʃ]	手錶
☑ check	[tʃɛk]	檢查
☑ umbrella	[ʌmˈbrɛlə]	雨傘
☑ kind	[kaɪnd]	仁慈

英語系列 : 62

躺著學美國口語1000

合著／蘇盈盈 , Lily Thomas
出版者／哈福企業有限公司
地址／新北市板橋區五權街 16 號 1 樓
電話／(02) 2808-4587 傳真／(02) 2808-6545
郵政劃撥／31598840　戶名／哈福企業有限公司
出版日期／2020 年 7 月
定價／NT$ 299 元 (附 MP3)

全球華文國際市場總代理／采舍國際有限公司
地址／新北市中和區中山路 2 段 366 巷 10 號 3 樓
電話／(02) 8245-8786　傳真／(02) 8245-8718
網址／www.silkbook.com 新絲路華文網

香港澳門總經銷／和平圖書有限公司
地址／香港柴灣嘉業街 12 號百樂門大廈 17 樓
電話／(852) 2804-6687 傳真／(852) 2804-6409
定價／港幣 100 元 (附 MP3)

封面內頁圖片取材自／shutterotook
email ／ welike8686@Gmail.com
網址／ Haa-net.com
facebook ／ Haa-net 哈福網路商城

國家圖書館出版品預行編目資料

躺著學美國口語1000 / 蘇盈盈, Lily Thomas合著. --
新北市：哈福企業, 2020.07

面；　公分. -- (英語系列；62)

ISBN 978-986-99161-2-7(平裝附光碟片)

1.英語 2.口語 3.會話

805.188　　　　　　　　　　　　109009724